'So you're n
involved with

Bella shook her head vehemently. 'I didn't say that. I'm just not going to lose myself in the process. And if I find someone, then he'll get a better bargain. Not some wimpy clinging vine.'

She smiled. 'I was getting a bit serious there. Sorry.'

He shook his head and captured her chin in his hand. 'You were telling me how you feel. And I'm privileged that you feel you can talk to me.' He let her go.

Their eyes met and there was silence for a moment as everything from the past seemed to shimmer between them. 'I've always felt I could talk to you,' she said.

MARRIAGE AND MATERNITY

Midwives in search of marriage and a family of their own . . .

For Abbey, Bella and Kirsten Wilson marriage and midwifery just don't mix.

Balancing work and home-life isn't on their agenda, because caring for each other and delivering babies to the women of Gladstone, New South Wales, is a full-time occupation.

It will take three very special men to persuade these three remarkable and dedicated women that they deserve marriage—and babies too.

A VERY SINGLE MIDWIFE

Midwife Bella Wilson is happy with her single status until gorgeous obstetrician Scott Rainford walks back into her life, and her heart...

Look out for Kirsten's story, coming soon in 2004 from Mills & Boon® Medical Romance™!

A VERY SINGLE MIDWIFE

BY

FIONA McARTHUR

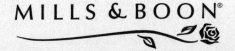

MILLS & BOON®

First published in Great Britain 2003
Harlequin Mills & Boon Limited,
Eton House, 18-24 Paradise Road, Richmond, Surrey TW9 1SR

© Fiona McArthur 2003

ISBN 0 263 83879 X

Set in Times Roman 10½ on 12 pt.
03-0204-45171

Printed and bound in Spain
by Litografia Rosés, S.A., Barcelona

CHAPTER ONE

Friday

THE birthing suite was quiet as Bella Wilson refilled the cup for Abbey to scoop ice chips as she needed.

Bella glanced across at her brother-in-law, Rohan, as he gently stroked his wife's back. Arched protectively around her on a low chair, his legs were either side of Abbey's thighs as she perched upright on the big blue ball. She rocked and moaned softly with the strength of the contractions and Rohan winced in sympathy with the sound.

Her sister's time was near. 'I'll ring Scott,' Bella whispered, and Rohan nodded. Nobody else seemed to notice the tremor in Bella's voice as she said it.

Although a very experienced midwife, Bella had chosen to be an onlooker at the time of birth rather than the person responsible for the safe arrival of the new Roberts baby. She wanted to see Abbey's face, and Rohan's, as her niece or nephew was born. She wanted to be a part of the whole experience and not just the mechanics of the birth. Scott should be the accxouchier.

Bella couldn't think of anyone she trusted more than Scott Rainford, Gladstone Hospital's Director of Obstetrics, to bring a baby into the world. Despite the fact there was still awkwardness between them, at least on Bella's side.

When she returned from the phone, Abbey's moans were a little louder and Bella went across to lay her hand on her sister's shoulder. 'It's OK, you're doing beautifully, nearly there.'

Abbey opened her eyes and stared at Bella as if to ground herself.

'I think I want to push.'

Bella nodded. 'Do what your body tells you to do.' Both women, as midwives, smiled at the litany and then Abbey's eyes widened as the feeling became stronger.

Rohan sat up straighter as he felt his wife tense with the change in sensation. 'You OK, sweetheart?'

Abbey nodded and Rohan rested his hands on her shoulders as if to transfer energy from his body into hers as she began second stage. 'I love you, Abbey,' he said, and kissed her shoulder.

Bella turned away. The strength of the bond between Abbey and Rohan brought tears to her eyes. She'd thought she had her chance at being a part of someone like that once, but now she believed that type of relationship wasn't for her. She could be strong on her own.

She heard the door open and there he was. The man who had once held her heart in his hands and let it go. Bella forced herself to meet Scott's eyes and their glances clashed before she turned back to Abbey.

The next contraction would be here soon and the birth was very close. She switched off all thoughts of Scott. 'Do you want the birth stool or are you going to move to the bed at the last minute, Abbey?' Bella hovered to help her sister when she'd made her choice.

'I'll sit on the bed, so I don't have to move afterwards.'

Bella nodded as she strained to hear Abbey's answer and lifted the beanbag onto the bed in readiness.

After the next pain, Abbey stood up and Bella and Rohan helped her onto the bed until she was sitting upright with her hands behind her knees. The next pain came swiftly and the baby's thatch of dark hair hovered at the entrance to the outside world before disappearing again.

'The baby took a look and went back,' Scott whispered, and they all smiled, though Abbey's smile was tired.

'I don't know how many times I've heard you say that over the years...' Her voice strengthened. 'Just didn't think I'd ever hear you say it to me.'

'One more push, Abbey.' Scott had always felt enormous admiration for the woman who had been midwife in charge until today, but during this labour Abbey had been inspiring with her belief in natural birth and her quiet acceptance of what her body required her to do.

'Here comes your baby,' Scott said quietly, and his heart constricted as the newborn eased into his hands as if the infant had finally decided it was time to arrive. Scott glanced at the clock as he gently lifted Abbey's baby up onto her stomach. 'Ten past three born. Wonderful, Abbey.'

A birth never failed to uplift him but when he looked at Bella and the joy in her face from this moment, it was as if the dam broke and his own loss overwhelmed him. He acknowledged the two things he'd most wished for in life would never be his. The woman he loved and the son he'd never met.

Scott heard Rohan let out a heartfelt sigh of relief that echoed around the room and it snapped him back into focus. As his medical partner and friend, Rohan had delivered hundreds of babies himself, but Scott could see that none had drained his friend like this.

'We have a son, Abbey.' Rohan's voice was thick with tears. His fingers stroked Abbey's cheek as if he still couldn't believe he'd been so blessed, and Abbey smiled up with a love and maternal joy that, despite its intimacy, shone to the darkest corners of the room.

Excluded, Scott had to look away as she decreed, 'We'll call him Lachlan.'

Bella smiled at the name Abbey had always fancied. There was something about that private glance shared between husband and wife that made Bella look at Scott, and for once the usually enigmatic Dr Rainford couldn't hide his bleakness.

Bella's heart squeezed at the look of raw pain in Scott's face, but then it was gone. He leaned forward to congratulate the parents and Bella was left with unanswered questions.

Questions for later, Bella thought as she kissed her sister, brother-in-law and precious dark-haired nephew, and returned to what she should be doing as the new midwife in charge. Euphoria at the safe arrival of Lachlan lightened her step as she bustled around and cleared the room of unneeded equipment. Abbey and Rohan deserved private time to share those precious early moments with their son and she would make sure it happened.

A fragment of her concentration tussled with possible reasons for Scott's depression as she pushed the green-draped trolley into the sluice room. Then she heard the sound of the doctor's footsteps as he followed her out of the delivery suite, and her fingers stilled.

'So you're the new unit manager now that Abbey has given birth earlier than anticipated?' Scott acknowledged the change in management but he didn't like it. He hadn't thought it through when he'd been told that Abbey's just-as-well-qualified sister would replace his midwife colleague during her maternity leave.

This last month he'd erected a wall between himself and Bella but now she was going to be in his face a lot more than he'd realised. Scott couldn't prevent the mocking note in his voice that he'd found was his only defence against this woman.

She turned to stare at him and shrugged delicately, and Scott could see the last glimmer of happy tears in her glorious lilac eyes. His heart contracted.

After yesterday's discovery of his full-grown son, today's birth was even more poignant. Perhaps if he hadn't pushed Bella away all those years ago he too would have had the opportunity to watch a son grow to a man. But having been proved a bad husband once, he'd chosen to let the young Bella go.

Bella had been eighteen and a virgin, to his thirty and divorced, and he'd felt a hundred. Freshly qualified in obstetrics, and new to town, he'd been so much under her spell he'd had to take drastic steps to protect her. He'd grown to love and respect Bella too much to risk her suffering the same pain he'd endured by marrying someone so much older than himself.

And today, to see Rohan and Abbey with everything that he desired, their happiness made the bleakness inside him crystallise into shards of pain that hardened on the outside. He felt old, which was the reason he'd never pursued the vibrant and beautiful Bella in the first place. Bella in his life, even a small amount, was a concept he needed to think about, something he couldn't do when faced with her.

She'd be hard to avoid now.

Bella's voice brought him back to the present and he'd missed the first part of her sentence.

'It was only a matter of days before Abbey was going on maternity leave anyway,' Bella said. 'Do you have a problem with me as Unit Manager, Scott?'

Her voice had always been gentle but lately he realised there was an underlying vein of inner strength that he'd never associated with Bella. He looked at her, slim and straight, and the top of her flame-red bun only came up to his throat—right where her presence caught him. He swallowed to clear away the tightness.

He'd no idea how he was going to cope seeing her every week day on the ward when all he wanted to do was carry her off to his house and lock her away from the big bad world that had tried to crush her.

Today's feelings, along with the hurt of realising his ex-wife had kept his son from him all these years, promised some painful hours of reflection in the coming weeks.

Too easily, he fell into his old defence mechanism of superiority until he could sort out this new relationship he'd have to deal with. 'I think you've taken on too much this time, Bella,' he said. 'Five days a week running the clinical and administrative side of the ward is different to working part time as the floating midwife.'

'Abbey managed it!' Bella sounded less confident than she should have but her older sister had always seemed to take responsibility in her stride.

'Abbey's an experienced manager,' he said, and made his escape before the emotion on her face and the emotions of the afternoon made him say something else he'd regret.

Bella stared after him and bit her lip. The man was insufferable, always had been, and she didn't know how Abbey had put up with him all these years.

Scott had been giving her, Bella, a difficult time since she'd started part-time orientation on the ward the previous month but it had never been as blatant as today. He'd almost vibrated with some inner rage and Bella hoped she was out of range when the eruption occurred.

He must be at least forty-two now, she supposed, though he looked much younger and as annoyingly handsome as he'd always been. Bella winced at the memory of the teenage infatuation she'd had for the gorgeous young doctor and, more painfully, his disclosure of her crush to Abbey after their mother had died. Even now, when she saw him, he flustered her just being there.

She really had been useless at love. There had been Scott, when she'd been eighteen. He'd seemed to return her feelings for an idyllic few months until she'd been mortified by his sudden change of heart.

Nursing had carried her through that rejection until she'd completed her midwifery.

Then she'd been pursued and won by the obstetrician she'd worked with in the birthing centre in Sydney. After three years of vague promises by Jason, he'd eventually admitted he'd been unfaithful from the start of their relationship and she'd run home. She certainly could pick them.

Finally, last year, she'd been drugged and the victim of a loathsome sexual attack by a vengeful old flame of Abbey's, which had almost destroyed the last vestiges of her self-worth. She'd wished the drug he'd slipped her had erased her memory of the attack and not just the strength to fight him off. That attack had been hard to come to terms with but out of the ashes of that experience had come her rebirth.

Somehow she'd conquered her fear and helped extricate them all when her attacker had returned to destroy Abbey. Dropping a plant pot on someone's head from upstairs didn't make Bella a heroine but it had had the desired effect! When the police had taken the man, Harrows, away, she'd felt the balance of power swing back her way.

She'd felt cleansed of the irrational but sapping guilt the attack had left her with. Instead of the usual scenario of big sister Abbey saving Bella—something Abbey had always done—Bella had saved Abbey! There was salvation in that thought and Bella had used it to drive herself to a new life.

She'd never be the champion her sister was, but she was learning to hold her own. And she would refuse to rely on a man for her happiness. So what Scott Rainford thought of her shouldn't matter.

Bella kicked a linen bag and the automatic kick-boxing hand posture that went with the kick made her laugh at herself. Her year of self-defence classes had turned out to be an absorbing challenge. She'd achieved many things in the last twelve months and Scott Rainford was not going to undermine her success with his bitterness.

She used that thought to insulate herself against the pricking pain she shouldn't be feeling from mere words. Furiously she cleaned the instruments and wiped the trolley down. He had no idea what she was capable of.

When Bella unlocked her front door it seemed a year since she'd left the house that morning. As she put down her bag, she realised that with all the excitement of Lachlan's arrival she'd forgotten she had to drive the youth bus tonight.

She stifled a sigh and hung her house keys on the hallstand. The chortling sound of a baby's laugh made her smile as she wandered into the kitchen.

'Your meal is on the stove, Bella.' Vivie, Bella's nineteen-year-old housekeeper, looked up from the last spoonful of vegetables she was trying to coax into her son's mouth. She grinned at Bella's appreciate sniff. 'I made your favourite. Pumpkin and macadamia soup. And congratulations on being an auntie.'

Bella ruffled the baby's hair and the little boy gurgled up at her. 'Thank you, Vivie. You're a treasure. I've just remembered I have two hours before my first bus trip. Do you want to slip up to see Abbey and baby Lachlan while I mind young Ro?'

Vivie's baby had been named after Abbey's husband, Rohan. They all shortened the baby's name to prevent confusion. Bella lifted the lid on the pot and closed her eyes as the soup's aroma filled the room. 'You should be a chef, Vivie. Your meals are fabulous.'

Vivie shook her head vehemently. 'I'm happy here, thank you. And I'd love to see Abbey and the baby for a few minutes if I could.' Vivie put the spoon down and wiped her son's mouth with his bib before she lifted him out and onto his play mat in the corner. 'We saw Rohan. He dropped in to see Aunt Sophie after he left the hospital. He looked pretty blown away by being a father.'

Bella smiled as she ladled soup into a bowl Vivie had left out for her. Rohan had a soft spot for Bella's elderly maiden aunt who resided in the front rooms of Bella's big house. An avid punter, Aunt Sophie's world revolved around her television set and penny-gambling on horse races via telephone.

'I'll take Aunt Sophie over to see them when they come home. She hates going out.' Bella smiled as she imagined her aunt's visit to Abbey and her baby in a few days. 'Who's home?'

Bella's family home had grown into a self-sufficient refuge for young women in crisis, something Abbey had unintentionally started before she'd moved next door with her new husband. Bella had expanded that aim when she'd taken over the house.

Vivie ticked off the people on her fingers. 'Melissa is still here, but she wants to go with you in the bus to the bowling club and needs to talk to you about a friend who wants to board.'

Bella looked up and mentally reviewed the rooms. There were three left. 'We'll see.'

Vivie nodded and went on. 'Lisa is still feeling unwell from morning sickness and is lying down, and Aunt Sophie said she's staying in her rooms until the last race. The twins have gone out but they did bring the washing in and put it away before they went.' She pushed the high chair back against the wall.

'Oh, and Dr Rainford rang and said he wanted to come on the bus with you tonight.'

The spoonful of soup on the way to Bella's mouth stopped in mid-air. 'Now, how the heck did he find out I was driving tonight?'

Vivie looked uncomfortable. 'He said he'd ring back when you got home and I mentioned you'd be in and out after seven. And it went on from there. Sorry.'

Bella put the untouched spoon back into the bowl and forced a smile. 'No problem. You go and see Abbey. Young Ro and I will stay here until you get back, then I'll get organised.'

Vivie smiled her thanks and dashed off to change. Bella lifted the spoon again. She did not understand how Scott Rainford thought he could barge into her private life uninvited. Why would he want to when he was obviously unhappy about her presence in his professional orbit?

It was five to seven and Bella had backed the cumbersome bus out of the garage into the driveway to allow her first passenger to board.

Melissa, at eighteen, was thirty-four weeks pregnant, and her yellow chenille trousers made Bella blink. Melissa's wrists jangled every time she moved her hands and her body piercing was nothing short of incredible. A sweet-natured girl, Melissa had been badly let down by the boyfriend she was still in love with.

'Vivie says you had something to ask me?' Bella smiled to convey that she was listening and waited for Melissa to explain. The girl drew a deep breath, as if preparing for the worst, and Bella looked back at her puzzled. 'Why so worried? I've never refused anyone in trouble, have I?'

'It's just that this is different. But not different! Well, it is different but shouldn't be.'

Bella blinked. 'Run that by me again.'

'My friend...' Melissa wrung her hands and the jewellery rattled and pinged with the movement '...is staying at the pub and it's expensive, and she's a really nice person. I guess, like me, the earrings and tattoos don't help people like them.'

'So you'd like your friend to stay at Chisholm Road until she finds somewhere to live. Is that right?'

Melissa twisted her hands again. 'Sort of. But different.'

Bella sighed. 'We're back to different. Different shouldn't be a problem.' She narrowed her eyes. 'Is she not pregnant, doesn't speak English, has two heads?'

'She's a he.' Melissa shot a glance at Bella and rushed on. 'His name's Blake, and he really is a sweetie.'

Bella stifled another sigh. She knew this had to come up some time. 'How old is your Blake?'

Melissa shook her head. 'He's not my Blake. I still

love Thomas.' Her head drooped. 'Even though he doesn't love me.' After a few moments of wishful thinking Melissa straightened her neck. 'But Blake is twenty and my very best friend. He hasn't been in town long but he stood up for me when some people were giving me a hard time and we've spent heaps of time together since. And I said I'd ask if he could stay. Maybe he could work around the yard or something. He said he would.'

Bella smiled at the girl in the rear-view mirror and reached across to shut the door. 'We'll see. We'd need a house meeting. I'm not promising anything.' She started the engine and the radio came on with the ignition and gave her a respite from further discussion. She needed to think about this.

At least she didn't have to deal with Scott Rainford while she worked it out. Bella wasn't sure whether she was relieved that Scott hadn't come or annoyed that she'd wasted time deciding what to wear. Relief won.

Unfortunately, just as she pushed in the clutch, his car drew up at the end of the driveway. Bella sighed and opened the passenger door again.

Darn. She could have done without this. Her pulse skipped and she closed her eyes for a second to steady her nerves.

He was dressed casually in dark jeans and a yellow polo shirt that sat snugly across his broad shoulders and deep chest. To Bella, he looked disturbingly handsome and charged with a virility that she could more easily ignore at work—but not tonight. He seemed bigger and stronger as he loomed over her seat and he made her aware of how slight she was compared to him.

'Were you leaving without me, Bella?' Scott had climbed the two steps into the bus and chosen the front seat directly next to her so that every time she turned her head she could see him. Bella wrinkled her brow. A faint drift of his expensive aftershave floated towards her and she resisted the temptation to breathe in more deeply. She had more sense than to lean towards self-destruction.

An enigmatic smile sat on his chiselled lips and his face was inscrutable. Bella reminded herself it was a waste of time to wonder what went on behind those cool green eyes of his. She never had been able to tell.

Maintain composure. Be assertive. She raised her voice over the radio. 'I wasn't waiting, Dr Rainford. Luckily you weren't late.' Bella put the vehicle smoothly into gear and pulled out into the street.

'You handle the bus well.' There wasn't any condescension in his voice but his comment annoyed Bella anyway. She turned the radio up a little more.

'Did you think I wouldn't?' she enquired sweetly as she negotiated a roundabout without touching the central island. She glanced across at his face and he was smiling. Now what was funny?

The laughter was in his voice. 'So, where are we going first?'

Bella sighed and turned the radio down a little. There was no use gaining a headache just to annoy Scott.

'It's a set route and we start at the south side of town and visit the clubs and pubs until we end up back where we started. First stop is Southside Bowling Club. Melissa is getting out there.'

Bella shut her mouth with a snap. Until someone got on, she would be alone with Scott as they drove around. And this was the quietest time of the night. Great.

'Why are you here anyway?' She listened to her own voice and the belligerence in it made her bite her lip. There was no excuse for bad manners. 'I'm sorry. That came out poorly.'

'Please, don't apologise. That's one of the reasons I'm here.' His words surprised Bella so much she reached over and turned off the radio.

Scott's smile was wry at the sudden silence in the vehicle and from the corner of her eye she saw him rub the back of his neck. So the great Dr Rainford was uncomfortable. Bella wasn't sure how that made her feel but it was good to know he wasn't one hundred per cent comfortable all the time.

Scott held his silence as they drew up to the bowling club and Bella flicked on the indicator and steered the minibus under the entrance portico. The door hissed open at the first stop and Melissa swayed belly-first down the aisle to carefully descend the steps. She turned back at the bottom step.

'You will think about it, won't you, Bella?' Bella nodded and the girl went on her way. The expression on Scott's face as he watched her leave made Bella smile.

When Melissa was out of earshot, he looked at Bella. 'Melissa makes me think of that Adam Harvey song about the girl who fell face first into the fishing-tackle box.'

'You're showing your age,' she said, and she saw him wince.

'That's because I'm old.'

The humour of the reply didn't quite come off and Bella shot him a look and changed the subject. 'So what was this about you apologising?'

His expression softened and Bella was surprised how good that made her feel. Danger lights flashed. She should not feel anything. Scott's hang-ups were no concern of hers.

He turned to face her fully. 'I'm not good at apologies so bear with me.' He took a deep melodramatic breath and his face was solemn.

'Bella Wilson, I...' he placed his hand over his heart with exaggerated sincerity '...Scott Rainford, apologise for any slur or aspersions I may have cast on your ability to run Gladstone Maternity Ward. It was uncalled for and inexcusable and not a true indication of my faith in your ability. Please, forgive me.'

Then he smiled. Bella looked into his eyes and it happened again. The world shifted and she knew he understood everything about her—just like that day twelve years ago when she'd fallen in love with him.

But she wasn't going there. She didn't need this. Bella fumbled with the gearstick until she found a gear and jerkily pulled away from the club as if to drive away would leave the words behind. She'd thought she'd sigh with relief when Scott stopped baiting her but now that he seemed so warmly approving she felt more off balance.

Even while she battled with the cumbersome bus in traffic, the awareness of Scott beside her didn't go away. The air in the bus seemed charged and no matter how much Bella berated herself for the resurgence of all those emotions she'd fought against as a teenager, she couldn't deny it—Scott's presence excited her.

Excited her in a way the three years with the permanently unfaithful Jason had never done. But excitement passed, she reminded herself, and she wasn't stupid enough to fall for that story again.

'Apology accepted,' she said quietly, and avoided his eyes.

Thankfully, the next stop saw two young women and a pimply youth board the bus and their friendly chatter helped distance the sensation that Bella was being drawn, inexorably, towards a fatal attraction she'd later regret. Because it wasn't going to happen!

Scott had also been quiet since that unmistakable awareness had passed between them. Bella had no idea of his thoughts. Perhaps he regretted he'd come tonight. Maybe now he'd apologised he'd go home after the run. She could only hope.

Bella dropped the three passengers at a noisy pub and the bus was empty again. 'After the next stop, I head home for nearly an hour before I do it all again.' She glanced at Scott and his eyes seemed to warm her from across the aisle. Her imagination was running away with her. Scott wouldn't look at her like that.

'It gets busier later in the evening.' Her voice cracked as she strove for normality and she wished he'd say something. Anything to break this mounting awareness that had come from nowhere and seemed to drain the strength from her body. She pulled into the last stop and two young blonde women, obviously twins, waved gaily as they clambered up the steps.

'Hi, Bella.' They looked at Scott curiously. 'Hello, Dr Rainford,' they chorused as they took their seats. Trish and Trina were just seventeen and Bella was pleased to see them heading home. Their mother was in hospital for a major operation and the girls had come to stay with Bella while she was away rather than with their stepfather whom they didn't get on with.

Bella glanced into the rear vision mirror. 'You ladies home for the night now?' The girls nodded.

Scott observed the interplay between Bella and the girls. She treated them with respect and yet he could see that she had a natural authority that came across despite the gentleness of her voice.

Authority was something he hadn't associated with Bella. This afternoon, after rational thought, he'd realised how badly he'd behaved to belittle Bella's ability to run the ward. If she'd been an unknown replacement for Abbey's job he would never have dreamed of undermining the new NUM's confidence. Just because he had a problem looking at Bella dispassionately he had no right to take it out on her. He'd always believed in fair play and in retrospect he'd been dismayed at his behaviour. They needed to let go of their past and establish a good professional friendship.

Then he'd found out Bella was driving the youth bus and the idea of her safety weighed on him as well. And a little aching curiosity about how Bella coped with young adults—people the same age as his son—something he didn't associate with beautiful but fragile Bella. Something he didn't associate with himself.

He shelved those thoughts for later. It was enough trying to remain rational around her.

Tonight had seemed a good opportunity to apologise for his lack of support at her promotion and see her in action. The trouble was, when he let his barriers down, the depth of his attraction to her swamped him like it had now and his plan of just being friends became difficult to stick to.

The bus pulled up at Bella's house more sharply than expected and everyone jerked in their seats. 'Sorry,' Bella murmured as she opened the door. The twins giggled as they waved goodbye.

Bella glanced at Scott. 'Are you on call for the ward?' Scott nodded and patted his pager and Bella raised her eyebrows. 'What were you going to do if your pager went off and they needed you in Maternity?'

'I was hoping the bus driver would drop me off. It's a small town.'

Bella smiled and his own lips curved. Hell, she was beautiful. She was still talking and he tried to concentrate.

'Are you going home now or were you planning to wait for the next run in an hour?'

Waiting with Bella would be exquisite torture but, now he realised there was a chance she'd be alone in the bus to pick up strange young people, he'd never settle at home. 'I'll wait.'

Bella glanced at him and he couldn't tell her thoughts from her noncommittal voice. 'Were you planning on coming on all the trips tonight?'

He avoided her eyes. 'I don't like the idea of you being here on your own.' He stood and watched her squeeze out from behind the wheel and waited for her to go past him before following her out. Her no-nonsense jeans hugged her tiny waist and stretched over the subtle curve of her buttocks and down her long legs like a second skin as she descended the steps. Scott closed his eyes.

At work he could control the direction of his thoughts. But tonight, after the decision he'd made today to get used to Bella being in his life again, it was much harder to stay detached.

In the old boarding-house-cum-family home it was quieter than he'd expected for just after eight o'clock in the evening. The bustling family atmosphere he'd vaguely assumed would distract him from lusting after Bella wasn't there. Now he was in trouble.

'Drop in and say hello to Aunt Sophie. She'd love to see you,' Bella said over her shoulder as she headed for the kitchen.

Scott glanced at the closed door in the foyer and accepted that the light streaming from under it meant that Sophie was awake. He knocked and a querulous voice called for him to enter.

The white-haired old lady was hunched in front of the television, watching the horse races as he'd expected, and she cackled softly when she saw him. Her bird-like face widened into a grin and he wondered not for the first time how she managed to eat with so few teeth.

'Bit late for a house call, Dr Rainford,' Sophie said.

Scott walked across the room to stand beside her chair. 'I'm doing the bus run with Bella tonight. How are you, Sophie? Keeping the house under control as usual?'

'Bella runs it. I just watch. And soon I'll see my new great-nephew.'

Scott smiled at the old lady's delight. 'He's a fine young fellow and Abbey looked wonderful when I saw her before tea.'

'They deserve their happiness. And so do you. You might think of doing something about it before you get too old.'

Scott raised his eyebrows but, in fact, nothing Bella's aunt said could surprise him after all these years of being her doctor. Sophie's eyes had strayed from his, back to the screen, as a new race started. He'd ceased to exist.

'Funny you should say that,' he murmured. More loudly, he said, 'I'll go, then. Good luck with your punting.'

She flicked him a sly glance. 'Good luck with yours.' And turned back to the television.

Scott bit back a sigh as he left the room. One thing about old age seemed to be that you could say what you wanted, when you wanted!

CHAPTER TWO

BACK in the foyer, the twins had disappeared up the stairs and then a barely audible thumping beat vibrated through the house. He looked down where the noise seemed to be seeping through the floorboards under his feet. Thump, thump, thump. He wondered if his son liked that kind of music and even if Bella did. He was definitely too old for Bella. He thought wistfully of his own quiet house until Bella returned from the kitchen and then age was forgotten.

She was munching an apple and he couldn't help the sudden connection in his head to Adam and Eve and the malicious serpent of desire. Even in jeans she embodied the essence of womanhood and he could feel the too-familiar surge of frustration at the unfairness of fate.

'It seems Vivie's gone to bed.' Bella said as she rubbed the uneaten side of her apple against her breast to shine it. Scott almost groaned at the undulation of tissue under the fruit. Oblivious, she went on, 'Her baby was unsettled last night and she's probably trying to catch up on some sleep.' Bella tilted her head and he could see she was unsure what to do with him. 'Do you want to listen to music in the study until the next trip?'

Scott tore his eyes away from the tightness of her shirt and dragged his thoughts back under control as he followed her into the book-lined room. He remembered the room they used as a study from when Abbey had lived here, but the aura was different.

Bella had painted the walls a soft lilac and replaced the old curtains with white linen. She gestured to an under-stuffed chair as she moved across to turn on the CD player. 'Please, sit down.'

Before he knew it Carol King had started to sing softly in the background about a life and a tapestry and he relaxed a little at the pleasant music. Bella crossed the room back to him as he sank into the chair. And sank comprehensively until his knees almost came up to his chin. He pretended to be comfortable though he felt like he'd been swallowed whole. At least it took his mind off Bella's breasts.

Bella perched on the arm of a sister chair and Scott could see why. Bella would disappear if she sank as far as he had.

Her eyes twinkled. 'Sorry about the chairs. There used to be a chaise longue in here but Rohan asked if Abbey could take it with her when they got married. Something to do with happy memories or something and I couldn't say no.' She grinned. 'He's so romantic and Abbey is so matter-of-fact. Love is grand if it works out.' She shrugged and patted the chair.

'I found these really cheap at a garage sale.' Her smile faded and she glanced out of the window at the house next door where her sister and brother-in-law lived. 'Poor old Rohan looked strained today while Abbey was in labour.'

She turned back to stare thoughtfully at Scott. 'And

so did you after the baby was born. What happened to a show of relief and joy at the birth of the new Roberts baby?'

She was different in her own home, more decisive and assertive, and it knocked Scott off balance. So much so that he answered by speaking about something he'd least intended. Something he hadn't told anyone since he'd found out yesterday.

'I was thinking about my own son.'

Bella blinked. 'You have a son? Since when?'

She looked so incredulous that Scott winced. 'It is possible, you know. I am a man.'

Bella snorted, not unlike her maiden aunt, and raised her eyebrows. 'I've been aware of that for a while.' And suddenly it was back—that aura between them that had shimmered in the bus. She blushed and looked away but not before he saw her moisten her lips with her tongue. That brief glimpse of pink softness almost undid all the hard work he'd expended on controlling his lust.

He rose, not without difficulty, from the softness of the upholstery, and walked over to the window. He had to move away or he'd pull her into his arms and do something he should have done many years ago.

He clung grimly to a topic that could divert him. 'As to "since when", a letter arrived from him yesterday. My son, Michael...' he shook his head as if still unable to believe he was a father '...apparently was adopted by his maternal grandparents not long after his birth, when his mother was killed in an accident. Until they died, and he came across his birth certificate, he didn't even know he had other parents.

He only mentioned that he'd discovered his real mother was long dead and the letter was to let me know my ex-wife had died. ''In case I wondered'', he added, and he might come to visit me in a month or two. He doesn't seem very keen to meet me.'

Scott turned back to Bella and the sympathy he saw in her face made him fiercely regret telling her. 'Considering I've done nothing for him, I'm not surprised, of course.'

Bella shook her head. 'If you didn't know about Michael then someone made it hard for both of you. Why didn't his mother tell you?'

'That's not something I'm ever likely to find out. We were totally different and never really understood each other. She probably thought I'd be as useless as a father as I was as a husband.' He saw her flinch at the bitterness in his voice. What did she expect? All those extra years he had on her were filled with mistakes.

Bella's voice was reasonable. 'As you're not useless at anything else you attempt, I find that hard to believe.'

'That's a compliment, considering I've been less than pleasant to you since you came back.'

Bella patted the chair and encouraged him to sit down again. 'We'll talk about that another time.' When he walked past her to his chair she touched his arm fleetingly and this time there was healing in her sympathy. To his relief she didn't pursue the subject.

Bella outlined a few changes she was looking at for the ward and the time passed swiftly. Before he knew it, she'd glanced at her watch and stood up. 'Let's go drive a bus.'

This time, as they circumnavigated the town, surprisingly there was little strain—on Bella's side anyway. More young people got on and off than the last trip and they all knew Bella.

Scott tried to concentrate on where they were driving and not the driver. He'd been aware of the bus campaign but was amazed at how much the service was used. No wonder the number of teen car accidents was down if this many kids weren't driving the streets.

When they returned to Bella's house the lights were out in Sophie's rooms. They were the only ones awake in a sleeping house and there was one more run to go. He felt his inner tension increase another knot and his steps slowed.

'Do you want to go back into the study and have some coffee?' Bella didn't appear to notice as she stifled a yawn.

Scott pictured another episode of trying to extricate himself from the carnivorous chair and, despite its diversional properties, he couldn't face it. 'Can we sit in the kitchen?'

Bella stared at him for a moment and the laughter in her eyes told him she'd guessed about the chair.

'Certainly.' She led the way into the old-fashioned kitchen and indicated a huge boiled fruit cake under a glass cover in the middle of the scrubbed oak table. 'I'll make coffee and you can cut us some of Vivie's cake. Then you can tell me about your marriage.'

She looked so innocent as she assumed he'd just

do as he was told and bare his soul. For some reason her assumption chipped a little more at his composure and he couldn't help his need to try and regain some control.

Bella wondered if she would get away with it. Hopefully Scott wouldn't take offence at her question. It would be nice to know more about the man she'd once thought she loved. Someone, she realised now, who'd always treated her like a child.

Without warning, he caught her arm as she moved towards the sink to halt her progress away from him. Apparently, Scott wasn't ready to discuss his marriage any further. It was the first time he'd touched her in twelve years and he wasn't touching her as if she were a child. Bella's pulse jumped with the unexpectedness of it.

'Who says I want to talk about my marriage?' His voice was deeper than usual with a touch of danger that accelerated her heart rate even more. 'You're being very bossy all of a sudden. When did this shift in power happen?' he asked with gentle sarcasm.

This was a startling side of Scott she'd never seen. Bella looked down at her own pale wrist captured by his much larger hand and then up at his face.

Her mouth was dry and she moistened her lips with her tongue, lost for words. Suddenly he was staring down at her like a dying man in a desert without water. The air crackled with tension and she could almost taste the scent of the storm to come.

She said quietly, 'Maybe I've changed and you've never noticed.' This time when she ran her tongue over her lips she did it to deliberately provoke him, but his response exceeded her expectations.

Bella felt his fingers tighten on her wrist even more and her eyes widened as he pulled her all the way towards him until she was hard against the rock of his chest with her head tilted up at him.

His voice lowered and the conversational tone he used belied the hungry look in his storm-green eyes. 'It drives me insane when you lick your lips. If you do it again I won't be responsible for the consequences.' Scott's fingers loosened and he dropped her wrist to sit down.

Bella blinked and pressed her lips together, rubbed her wrist and turned away. Her mouth was dry, and a heaving, almost sickening excitement she didn't want to feel coursed through her stomach as she filled the kettle. At least she'd found out the tiger's tail could be pulled, she thought shakily.

When she returned to the table with the mugs of steaming coffee, Scott had cut two pieces of cake.

A tiny green flame simmered in his eyes and Bella threw up her chin at the challenge—something the Bella of a year ago would never have done—and she gloried in it. 'So, does this mean you don't want to talk about your first wife?'

Scott's hand froze as he reached for his cup.

Ha. Good, she'd surprised him, she thought with sudden satisfaction, and for once she could read his mind. 'You really haven't seen how much I've changed since the court case, have you?'

Scott paled and clenched his teeth as he fought back the impotent fury that invaded his mind whenever he thought of Bella at the drugged mercy of her attacker. He took a deep breath. 'We seem to have successfully avoided each other for most of the last year since you've been home. I didn't get the impression it helped you when I was around.'

She shrugged delicately and her fragility belied the strength in her voice. 'They say good comes out of even the worst scenarios. That experience taught me to rely on myself and not other people. And not to expect my big sister to always save me. I've worked on that over the last year.'

Scott frowned. 'To say good came out of a brutal attack seems a tad forgiving of a creep who drugged and abused you.'

Bella winced with distaste and her voice shook a little. 'He can rot in gaol, but surviving his attack has forced me to grow and learn. You weren't here straight after the attack, but for a while I was ready to crawl away and die.'

Scott had shut off a lot of the memories of Bella's attack because he'd felt so useless in her hour of need. He'd been away and had come back to find a shattered shell of the woman he'd known. She'd refused to see him when he'd come to offer comfort so he'd gone away again and gained what reassurance he could from information gleaned from Rohan. Scott felt he'd already hurt her enough all those years ago to feel he had the right to push his presence on her when she was vulnerable.

'But I don't want to talk about me, I want to hear about you…' She trailed off and managed a small smile of encouragement.

He smiled grimly. 'So it's my turn, is it?' He could see that she'd sat far enough along the table away from him to be out of reach. At least he'd made her wary but it hadn't stopped her impudence.

'How old were you when you were married?' The question drifted towards him and he would have liked to know why it was so damned important for her to hear this. He considered refusing to answer but he never had been able to deny Bella anything if she wanted it badly enough.

His voice was expressionless. 'Married at twenty, but she left less than a year later. Pretty well most of med school was spent trying to forget my marriage. We fell in and out of love very quickly. Or at least she did.'

Scott could see the brevity of his answer irritated Bella and it gave him a little satisfaction that she could be frustrated for once.

'Then why get married?'

'I was young and stupid and she was older and no wiser. It blew incredibly hot and then, before I knew why, our relationship was as cold as ice. She left me for another man, a man her senior who could support her, and filed for divorce.' A distant echo of a crushing hurt was in his voice and Bella felt more mature than Scott for the first time in her life. It was an interesting concept.

Luckily he wasn't looking at her. His voice was flat when he went on, 'Apparently my wife was pregnant when she left me. I just wish I'd known I had a child and could have been involved in some part of his life. The last two days I've agonised over why she shut me out so completely. I rang and checked. I am Michael's true father.'

He shrugged. The image of the pain in Scott's face in the birthing suite that morning came back to her. 'And you've learnt nothing else about your son?'

'What's there to learn? He's a man now. I imagine from his side I'm the father who's done nothing to help him. It must be more of a shock to him than it was to me.'

Bella drained her coffee and set the cup down. She glanced at the clock on the kitchen wall. 'It's almost time for the bus run again.'

Scott gave her a wry smile and stood to pull out her chair. 'Well, that will end our session of truth and dare for the night. Thank goodness.'

'It's not healthy to keep all this stuff bottled up, Scott.' Bella was stern in her new role. 'When the shock wears off, you'll be glad you told me.'

'Right,' Scott said cynically, and waited for her to precede him out of the room.

When they'd settled in the bus and Scott saw Bella stifle another yawn his original misgivings came back to him. 'This is ridiculous. You shouldn't be driving this bus. Can't you find someone else to do it?'

Bella shook her head. 'The government has promised funding for next year. That includes the employment of a salaried driver. I can survive until then.'

'But why is it your problem?'

Bella shrugged. 'Because if I didn't do it, no one else would. I agree with my sister in the basic goodness of the younger generation. The advantages of the service are worth the effort.'

The conversation came to a halt because the bus had reached the first stop. A large group of young men and women clambered on and the noise level in the bus made conversation between Bella and Scott impossible, which was OK because he had enough to think about. Not the least was how soft Bella had felt in his arms and how hard it had been to let her go. Her support for his dilemma with his son was also surprisingly comforting.

At each stop the bus became more crowded until finally people started to get off and head home. By the time Bella had arrived back at Chisholm Road there were only Melissa and a young man left.

Bella had glanced in the rear-view mirror a few times. Blake—Bella assumed it was the Blake Melissa had befriended—had a sweet smile and laughter-filled eyes. In fact, Bella had liked him on sight.

When they moved to the front of the bus to alight, Melissa's pleading eyes left Bella in no doubt of the young man's identity.

'This is Blake, Bella.'

Bella swivelled in her seat and held out her hand. Blake's long brown hair looked clean and his goatee was interesting, though she wasn't sure if she was thrilled with the small scorpion tattooed on his wrist or the skull and crossbones piercing his eyebrow. Scott's going to love this, she thought.

She met the young man's green eyes and nodded. 'Hello, Blake.' Blake shook Bella's hand. 'This is Dr Rainford.' The two men nodded at each other but neither held out their hand. Bella smiled wryly to herself.

'Perhaps you could come and see me tomorrow and we can discuss Melissa's idea.'

Blake nodded. 'Thank you. I will.' He glanced at Scott once more and then followed Melissa out of the bus, where they went into a huddle for a minute before he headed off down the street.

Bella realised she'd been swayed to coolness by the fact that Scott was there, and the thought irritated her.

'What was all that about?' Scott's timing was way out.

'Nothing important.' She put the bus into gear and reversed it carefully down the driveway. 'Let's get this bus parked. I'm tired. It's been a long day.'

He waited until she switched off the engine in the garage before pushing his luck. 'For nothing important, there was a lot of eye contact going on all round. What does he want?'

Bella stifled a sigh and measured her answer. 'Blake has offered to do odd jobs around the house in exchange for lodging. I'm thinking about it.'

Scott frowned and shook his head. 'I can do odd jobs around the house. I don't think introducing a young man as a boarder is a good idea.'

Bella held back the comment that it was none of his business. Her voice was sweet. 'And here I was thinking that having a large country medical practice and most nights on call would be enough to keep you busy. I must start a list of repairs for you.'

She stood up and eased herself from her seat. 'Goodnight, Scott.'

He followed her out and towered over her beside

the bus. 'I enjoyed your company, Bella. We must do it again.'

'Any Friday and Saturday night,' Bella said dryly, and walked away.

Scott's firm voice drifted across. 'Then I'll see you at seven tomorrow night.'

Bella thought of those moments in the kitchen and how much she had cared about Scott's distress over his son. She closed her eyes and didn't look back. 'I don't think that's a good idea,' she whispered to herself.

CHAPTER THREE

Saturday

'BELLA, Blake's here.' Melissa's voice drifted from the front door. Bella put down the morning newspaper and stood up from the kitchen table. She met Vivie's eyes and Vivie shrugged.

At breakfast, Bella had spoken to Aunt Sophie about the possibility of a male boarder and her aunt had sent the ball back into Bella's court with a non-committal shrug. 'If he's likeable and honest, it's not a bad thing to have a man about the house,' she'd said.

All the other girls except Vivie had met Blake previously and thought it 'cool' that he might move in with them. Bella had had to bite back a smile as they'd unanimously agreed to hand the mowing and the garbage-bin duties over to him if he joined the household.

Bella walked into the hallway and smiled at Blake. 'Come through into the kitchen, Blake, and we'll have a coffee and see if we can work something out.'

Blake shot a glance at Melissa who nodded encouragingly and hung back to watch them go.

Vivie brought the coffee-pot over and when they were all seated at the kitchen table, Bella looked across at the young man. Tall and good-looking under the ponytail and eyebrow stud, there was something about the square chin under his goatee that invited a smile.

She couldn't help but like him. 'You haven't met Vivie, have you, Blake?'

Blake smiled at the young woman. 'Hello, Vivie.'

Vivie nodded but didn't say anything.

'Vivie runs the house. She shops and is a fabulous cook and we're very lucky to have her. That's why she's in on this discussion.' Vivie blushed and looked down at the tablecloth.

Bella moved on. 'If we were to think about inviting you to move in, Blake, it's only fair that we'd run through the expectations we have for everyone in the household.'

Blake nodded that he understood.

Bella continued, 'Melissa said you might be willing to do some odd jobs around the house.'

Blake shrugged. 'I don't have employment at the moment, and I get bored if I'm not busy. I'd enjoy the chance to do some work around here. In Sydney I worked for the Salvation Army Depot and restored furniture, so I can fix most things.'

Bella nodded and considered his answer. 'Why did you move to Gladstone?'

He grimaced. 'When my parents died I went off the rails a bit. The guys I was with started to get into some heavy stuff and I didn't want to go there.' He looked embarrassed. 'I thought it might be a good idea to leave town while I could still drive away. I ended up here.'

Blake smiled sheepishly. 'I thought if I went to a country town there was more chance of a fresh start.

I like the idea of moving into the house.' He couldn't keep the anxiety out of his face.

Bella held out her hand. 'We'll go for a week's trial and we've room for another car in the garage besides the bus. My car's just died a decrepit death and it can be relegated to the back shed.'

Blake smiled a huge smile and he didn't notice that Vivie looked ready to pass out with the brilliance of it. 'You could drive mine. Maybe I could fix yours, too. I like mucking around with cars.'

'Don't give yourself too much to do or we'll miss you if you decide to move out.' Bella smiled. 'Welcome to the house, Blake.'

She looked at Vivie. 'Would you like to show Blake his room? He can have the end room at the back of the house. That one has its own bathroom, even though it's pretty rough.' She looked at Blake with a challenging stare. 'You clean your own bathroom every week. We don't do men's rooms.'

'I'll show you how.' Vivie managed to enter the conversation finally. 'When you get your stuff I'll make the room up for you—then it's up to you. You get clean sheets on a Friday.' Vivie had moved into housekeeper mode and Blake followed her out of the room.

Bella could hear Vivie explaining about mealtimes and how he had to tell her if he wasn't planning on being there for a meal. It would do Vivie good to have some male company other than her year-old son, Bella thought with a smile. Vivie had been on the receiving end of a bad experience, like Bella herself, and she needed to practise her feminine wiles. Bella had decided she didn't need her wiles.

*   *   *

Later Bella was stepping out of her front door for the first bus run of the evening when Scott fell into step beside her.

'Good evening, Bella. Here we are again,' he said.

'So I gather. Hello, Scott.' She looked up at him. 'This really isn't necessary you know.'

'Humour me,' he said as they walked together towards the garage.

Bella sighed and waited for the fireworks. She stepped past a fire-engine red, low-slung, two-door SLR Torana with silver mag wheels and BITE ME splashed across the front windscreen. Scott's eyes widened as he followed Bella onto the bus.

'Where on earth did that car come from?' Scott twisted his neck and screwed up his face in disgust.

Bella settled herself into the seat before she answered and didn't look across at her passenger. 'It's Blake's car. He moved in today.' She started the bus's engine and revved it. It was a diesel engine and she shouldn't do that before it warmed up, but the motor's noise successfully drowned out Scott's reply.

Scott glared across at her. When the engine was back at an idle he tried again. 'Does Abbey know you now have a male boarder?'

Bella could feel the elevation in her blood pressure. At least she assumed that was what the red mist in front of her eyes meant. 'Excuse me?' She turned to Scott and spoke softly but the edge was unmistakable. 'Perhaps you'd like to trot up to the hospital and tell my sister while she's breastfeeding. I can't wait for her to tell you it's none of her business.' To reinforce her point she opened the door again and waited.

Scott met her eyes and raised his eyebrows at her reaction. 'That's not what I meant, but I'm sorry if I upset you.'

Bella said nothing. The door closed again and she put the bus into gear and drove out of the garage.

Scott held his peace as they drove the circuit but mentally he gnashed his teeth. He couldn't believe she'd been so reckless and invited some unknown youth into her house. And judging by his car, the boy was loud and a hothead as well. Scott remembered the boy's pierced eyebrow and tattoo and clenched his fists. If anything happened to Bella he'd grind the pipsqueak into a pulp.

They didn't talk much during the first trip. There were a few more young adults than last night's early trip and Bella was kept busy stopping and starting the bus.

By the time they were back at Bella's house she had calmed down enough to accept she might have overreacted and Scott was being careful.

They almost made it to the next bus run as they talked of ordinary things and then suddenly, as they stood up to leave, it was as if he couldn't restrain himself. Scott threw in a contentious question.

'So where does Blake sleep?' The words hung in the air between them.

Bella blinked and raised her eyebrows. How dared he? 'That's funny.' She tilted her head. 'I was under the impression that the guests in my house had nothing to do with you.'

She glared but this time Scott stared back without expression and wouldn't be silenced. 'It's not unreasonable for your friends to be concerned if we consider you've made an ill-judged decision.'

'Ah,' said Bella. The red mist was coming back. 'Patronising! That's the Scott we all know and love.'

Scott glared back. 'Don't avoid the issue. You're just asking for trouble. You can't know anything about this person. What if he tries to break into your room in the night? He could have a criminal record as long as your arm. I'm concerned for you, Bella.'

'I like him and I trust my instinct.'

'Abbey trusted her instinct with Clayton Harrows and look where that led both of you.'

'How dare you?' Bella couldn't believe he'd brought her sister's ex-fiancé into the conversation. She'd just managed to get those memories of her attack back in their box after last night, and he was opening the lid again. She couldn't believe it. Where did this man get off?

Scott wasn't repentant. 'I dare because I care.'

'So what changed you to care?' The bitterness in her voice made Scott wince. He couldn't help the step he took towards her and before he knew it he had her pulled against him.

He looked into her eyes and his voice was barely audible. 'I've always cared!'

She smelt of some herbal shampoo and flowery perfume that triggered the response he'd been fighting against all night, and his body quickened with desire and a stupid jealousy that she believed some twenty-year-old over him.

Oblivious to the tightening of his fingers, Bella tossed her hair and glared back at him. This was a Bella he'd never seen. 'Big effort, Scott. Be careful, or someone will hear you,' she taunted. 'I have to watch what I say in case you run to Abbey with it, like you did when I was eighteen.'

The bitterness in her reply shocked them both. Scott lowered his voice. 'I "ran to Abbey" to protect you. Don't you realise? I was *twelve years* older and you were only eighteen. I couldn't trust myself.'

'So what's changed now?' This was crazy and needed to stop. Bella could hear the scorn in her own voice and she consciously relaxed her shoulders and attempted to step back.

But it was too late.

Scott pulled her against him and lowered his face. His eyes burned into hers as he captured her chin firmly in his hand so she couldn't step away again.

When his lips touched hers they seared then softened and he sighed into her. Bella tasted a mixture of anger and regret and a glimpse of incredibly sweet homecoming that seemed to settle over her like a fine warm fog, and it was tantalisingly delicious. The room swam before her eyes as she leaned into him. To be in Scott's arms was everything she'd been afraid it would be.

This feeling was too dangerous after all she'd been through. Bella didn't want to go there—not without thought. She turned her face to break the spell, shrugged out of his hold with a practised move she'd gleaned from her self-defence classes and backed away so that he stepped back too.

'I'm sorry,' he said. 'I shouldn't have come tonight.' The words were clipped, as if he was still striving for control. 'I'd better go.'

This was like a nightmare. Here she was, wanting

Scott to kiss her so she could open herself up to pain a fourth time. 'Please, do,' was all she said.

Bella stood ramrod straight in front of him and full of purpose. She'd grown up and he hadn't seen it until now. She didn't need protecting by anyone. Not even by him.

Bella glanced at her watch. 'I'm quite capable of doing the trips on my own.'

He nodded. 'I can see that. Goodnight, Bella.'

'Goodnight, Scott.' Bella watched him go and now she was more confused than ever. She wasn't quite sure where all that emotion had come from but it had better get back where it came from because she was finally self-sufficient and happy. The last thing she needed to do was get tangled up in some angst-filled relationship with Scott Rainford so that he could get cold feet again and break her heart a second time.

Later that evening, Bella had just crawled into bed when someone knocked quietly on her door. Her heart jumped and for a moment her chest felt heavy with panic. Scott's dire warnings about Blake still rung in her ears until common sense told her it was probably one of the girls.

'Yes?' It was more of a squeak than an enquiry. She sat up and cleared her throat to try again. 'Who is it?'

'It's Blake.'

Bella couldn't help the hand that flew to her chest. It was as if Scott was at her shoulder saying, *See*. The feelings she'd conquered a year ago echoed in her memory. She steadied herself. She mustn't jump to conclusions.

Bella drew a deep breath to steady her nerves and deliberately padded across to the door and opened it slightly.

'What do you want, Blake?' She couldn't help the snap in her voice but then she saw the concern in his face and realised he posed no threat to her. Damn Scott Rainford for putting those suspicions in her head.

'It's Melissa. She thinks she's in labour.'

Bella nodded and opened the door wider. 'I'll just get my dressing-gown.'

When they'd moved down the hallway to the girl's room they found Melissa sitting wide-eyed and trembling on the edge of the bed.

Bella sat down beside her. 'What's wrong, Melissa?'

Melissa grabbed Bella's hand for comfort. 'It's the backache, and it keeps coming and going. It wasn't too bad earlier but in the last half an hour it's coming much quicker and now I'm getting these bad cramps in the front, too.' She looked up at Bella with frightened eyes. 'Do you think it might be labour?'

Bella smiled wryly. 'It certainly sounds like it. Why didn't you come and see me earlier?'

'I didn't think you were home and it wasn't so bad before...' The girl stopped and her face contorted with pain. Bella laid her hand on Melissa's abdomen and the hardness of the uterus under her fingers confirmed the contraction. She shut her eyes for a second while she thought of what they had to do.

'The contractions are strong. We need to get you up to the hospital to see if we can stop your labour.'

'What if my baby is born today?' There was real fear in Melissa's voice.

Abbey hugged the girl. 'We'll have to see how big he or she is. Some thirty-four-weekers have few problems but most need special care for several weeks. It's mainly the poor feeding that will keep your baby from coming home as quickly as a full-term baby. Now, let's get you organised.'

She looked up at Blake. 'Thanks for getting me, Blake.' She glanced around the room. 'At least we packed Melissa's hospital bag last week.'

The young man looked less worried now that Bella was there to take command, but his anxiety wasn't over as Melissa grabbed his hand.

'Come with me, Blake. Thomas won't come, and I'm scared.'

Blake backed away and he looked at Melissa with reluctance. 'Are you sure you want me? Bella will be with you. You'll be fine.'

Melissa's eyes implored him. 'I want you, too. Please.' Bella watched the interplay. Whatever was best for Melissa was fine by her.

Blake swallowed the lump in his throat and nodded. 'OK. If you think it will help you, Melissa.'

He looked at Bella. 'What do you think?'

'You can stay up at the head end of the bed, Blake,' Bella reassured him with a smile. 'Just hold her hand and tell she's doing a great job. That's all you have to do.'

Bella left a note for Vivie in the kitchen on their way out to say where they'd gone.

'We'll have to take the bus,' she said as she remembered her car was out of action.

'Take mine. I'll drive.' At least Blake felt confident about getting them there.

Bella nodded and helped Melissa into the front. She stifled a grin at what Blake would do if Melissa's waters broke all over his luxurious lambswool seat covers. In fact, she would have preferred to have her first drive in a hot rod in a less stressful situation and without Blake's lead foot, she thought as the houses flashed past.

The upside was it only took them five minutes to get to the hospital, though they'd probably wakened the neighbourhood.

When they arrived at Maternity, the ward was busy with a woman in labour in the other birthing unit. Rather than short-staff the night girls, Bella admitted Melissa to the ward and settled her into bed. Blake sat on the chair beside Melissa and held the young girl's hand.

With the night staff so busy it fell to Bella to ring Scott. Bella sighed as she dialled his number and listened to it ring. So much for avoiding Scott.

'Hello?' Considering it was after midnight, he sounded wide awake.

Sunday

Bella's mouth was suddenly dry and her voice came out huskily. 'Scott, it's Bella.' Before he could think she'd rung him for personal reasons, Bella hurried on. 'I'm at Maternity with Melissa. She's in labour at thirty-four weeks and I'd say she's well established.'

There was a couple of seconds' silence as he processed the information and then he said, 'I'm on my way,' and put the phone down.

Bella replaced her own receiver gently and turned to Melissa. 'He's coming in now.'

'That's good.' Melissa's voice was faint. 'Because I think my waters just broke and these contractions are getting pretty bad.' She met Bella's eyes and tears welled up and overflowed. 'Will my baby be OK?'

Bella hugged the girl. 'Your baby will be fine.'

'I don't think I can do this any more.' Melissa's eyes were wild as she glanced at Blake, then at Bella, and then around the room as if to find a place to hide from the strength of the contractions.

Bella nodded and soothed her. 'I know. The contractions are very strong and it is hard. You're doing wonderfully.'

'You are, too,' Blake said loudly, as if he'd just remembered his lines.

Bella hid her smile as she turned on the foetal monitor and they all listened to Melissa's baby's heart sounds gallop along merrily. 'How about Blake goes outside for a moment and I'll check to see how dilated you are? If there's absolutely no chance that your labour will stop, you can jump in the shower. To stay lying down in bed makes the pain harder to bear.'

Despite the abdominal palpation she'd done, Bella wanted to confirm that the baby's head was coming first as well as check there was no cord prolapse after the waters had broken, though that scenario seemed unlikely with the strong foetal heartbeat they'd just heard.

'The shower sounds like heaven,' Melissa agreed.

*   *   *

Scott pulled up outside Maternity and the lecture he'd given himself, about maintaining composure around Bella, flew out the window as he saw *that* car parked outside. He glared at it and stalked up the stairs. The boy had already ruined one young girl's life with a pregnancy, and now he'd latched onto Bella. Well, *he* was watching him.

Sharon, one of the night midwives, met him at the door and took one look at his grim expression.

'You OK, Scott?'

'Fine.' He eased the scowl from his face and loosened his shoulders. 'I was thinking about something else.' He gestured to the two birthing suites. 'Which way first?'

'See Bella and then we're ready to have this baby in number one,' Sharon said as she peeled off to answer the buzzer from her own unit.

Scott nodded, plastered a neutral expression on his face, and went in to see Melissa.

'So, it's all happening, Melissa.' They all looked up with relief when Scott walked in. He could tell things were progressing fast and when Bella handed him the chart he glanced at her findings and nodded. He looked at Blake under his brows but didn't say anything. Bella had confirmed that Melissa's cervix was nine centimetres dilated and it was only a matter of time before her baby would be born.

Bella placed the ultrasound Doppler over Melissa's stomach. The strong beat echoed around the room and everyone smiled. 'He or she sounds happy about arriving early,' Scott reassured his patient, and Melissa smiled weakly back until the next pain arrived.

'I'd like to get Melissa into the shower until she's ready to push, if that's OK with you, Doctor?'

Scott grimaced. 'All you Wilson girls are the same. Nobody likes to look after people on the bed any more.' He waved them on. 'Try to be back here before we have a head on view. Sharon has the nursery ready if we need a crib. I'll go next door and see how they're doing.' He nodded at Melissa and Bella, ignored Blake and left.

Blake hung back as Bella encouraged the girl out of bed but Melissa was having none of it. 'You come, too.'

Bella bit her lip at Blake's discomfort but then she saw him accept that it was boots-and-all commitment if he was going to help Melissa. He went up another notch in Bella's estimation.

'OK.' His voice firmed. 'If I can help, just ask.' He followed them into the bathroom.

Bella helped Melissa to sit on the big blue ball in the bathroom and as soon as the hot water hit her lower stomach she sighed with relief. Bella could see the tension drain from her shoulders and made Blake sit behind her to gently rub the girl's lower back in a circular motion.

After an initial awkwardness, Blake settled into a soothing rhythm and Bella could see it helped Melissa. 'You're both doing wonderfully. Stay loose and it will all happen.'

The lights were dim and the sound of the running water was peaceful between contractions as they waited for Melissa's baby to start its descent through the birth canal.

Within half an hour Melissa stood up and the

change in her breathing was clearly audible to Bella. 'I need to push,' Melissa panted, and Bella nodded.

'Listen to what your body is telling you to do. Don't be frightened. It's OK.'

Melissa couldn't help the involuntary downward pressure she was exerting and she squeezed Blake's hand as she pushed. 'I can feel it move,' she whispered. Blake paled and stepped back to let Bella closer.

'It's OK. Have a rest when the pain is gone.' Bella placed the tiny waterproof Doppler low down on Melissa's stomach and the clop-clop of baby's heartbeat echoed clearly in the bathroom.

'Your baby's still happy.'

'I'm not,' said Melissa.

Bella smiled and squeezed her hand. 'You are magnificent!'

Blake nodded in total agreement.

'Here comes another one...' Melissa gritted her teeth and Bella stroked the girl's jaw.

'Loose jaw, loose perineum, Melissa. Remember that all the power is travelling down and not to waste it in your face or arms.'

Melissa consciously relaxed her face and then her eyes widened. 'I think it's coming.'

Bella ran her gloved hands between Melissa's legs and sure enough a tiny bulge of baby's head had descended enough for her to feel. 'Well done, Melissa. It would have taken heaps more pushes than that if you'd stayed on the bed.' Bella glanced at the door.

'OK. We'd better shuffle back to the bed and keep the doctor happy.' As soon as the pain was gone, Bella cajoled Melissa into movement and Blake and

Bella supported her to the bed. Bella pressed the call button and Scott and the night sister appeared within seconds.

When Melissa had climbed onto the bed everyone could see how close the baby was to arriving and Scott met Bella's eyes with a shake of the head as if to say, Too close.

Bella smiled sweetly in return and settled Blake back into the chair because he looked like he was ready to faint.

She could hear Scott washing his hands as she gave Blake a drink of water and the whistle of the oxygen as Sharon checked the infant resuscitation trolley. It was all happening very quickly.

'Gently now,' Scott murmured as his gloved hand rested lightly on the baby's head and Melissa whimpered. The sound made Blake squeeze Melissa's hand and put his cheek next to hers. 'You're nearly there. You're so clever and you get to see your baby soon.'

She nodded that she understood. Bella left them to it and watched the birth.

With aching slowness, Melissa's pelvic floor guided her baby's body through the twists and turns required to reach the outside world. The mechanisms of birth never failed to awe Bella. Her years in Sydney at the birthing centre had reinforced her belief that in the great majority of cases, a woman's body would achieve what it had to if the mother believed in herself.

The back of the baby's head extended to allow the forehead, nose and chin to be born in one sweep of the perineum and, with little delay, its head restituted to allow the shoulders under the pubic arch, followed by the rest of its body, and the infant came into the world in a slithery rush.

Scott lifted the baby up to show Melissa. 'Brilliant job, Melissa. Well done. So, what have you got?' he asked.

Melissa opened her eyes and stared up at the diminutive baby. 'Oh, it's a girl and she's so tiny. I want to call her Tina.'

Blake's eyes were shining with unshed tears as Scott laid Melissa's daughter on her mother's breasts.

'Hello, Tina,' Bella said as she tucked a bunny rug around them both while Scott clamped the cord.

'Do you want to cut the cord?' Scott asked Blake in a noncommittal voice.

Blake shook his head. 'I'm not the father.'

Scott blinked in surprise.

'Do it anyway,' Melissa whispered, and Bella could see Blake steel himself for a task he didn't relish. He took the scissors Scott handed him in shaky fingers and sawed his way through the sinewy tissue. When Tina was finally separated from her mother, Blake put the scissors down. Any remaining colour drained from his face, his eyes rolled and he flopped bonelessly back into the chair.

Bella stifled a smile and gently directed his head down to his knees and held him there until he groaned. 'What happened?' he mumbled.

'You were a bit faint. Stay there for a minute. You'll be fine.' She caught Scott's contempt when he raised his eyebrows as if to say, What do you expect? Bella glared back at him and his face crinkled with amusement at her predictable reaction.

Bella blinked. He was teasing her. It wasn't something she was used to from Scott and a small unwilling smile tugged at her mouth.

Sharon leant over to listen to the baby's heart and breathing and pronounced her fine. Because of Tina's early arrival they would still keep her in the crib overnight.

It took another hour for Melissa to be showered, see Tina settled into her humidicrib and then be tucked into her own bed. Finally she was settled enough to let Bella and Blake go.

Back at Bella's house, Vivie was up despite the fact that it was barely four a.m.

Blake was still blown away by the experience of childbirth and couldn't wait to share his excitement about the night's events. 'I think what Bella does for a job is amazing. Imagine being responsible for the safety of a baby so small.' He rolled his eyes. 'You all looked so calm!'

Bella smiled. 'Being a midwife is the best job in the world. We get to look after all the things that happen naturally. If you want pressure, you take the doctor's side of it and it's their job to come in when things start to go wrong. It gets a bit tense then.'

'I suppose so,' Blake didn't look like he was ready to go to sleep yet and Bella hid her yawn. Thank goodness it was Sunday today and she could sleep in. This week was going to be a big one at work and she wanted to be refreshed for it. Blake would probably buzz for hours. Vivie didn't seem in a hurry so she could keep Blake company. Bella stood up.

'I'm sorry, Blake. I have to go to bed. I'll see you later on.' Bella carried her cup to the sink and yawned again.

Blake jumped up. 'I'll wash them. Vivie said if I use anything in the kitchen, I have to wash it up. So I'd better do it.'

Bella met Vivie's eyes and they both grinned. 'I think that's a good idea,' said Bella, tongue in cheek, and took herself off to bed.

But she couldn't sleep. How could so much have happened in so short a time? Apart from tonight's birth, she had a new nephew, was in charge of a ward, in charge of a bus, in charge of a house with their first male boarder and now Scott was intruding in her life when she didn't need the distraction.

The kiss between them earlier had stolen some of her hard-won calm. The feel of his lips against hers, the weight of his hand holding her against the hardness of his chest, his breath mingling with her own. It had been heady stuff and something she'd refused to speculate on in the year since she'd moved back to Gladstone. She really didn't think she would survive another emotional disaster. She'd just have to refuse to let him distract her.

CHAPTER FOUR

Monday

WHEN Bella pulled up for work on Monday morning
in Blake's car, she had a silly grin on her face from
the rumbling and roaring sound the car made as it
drove along.

Heads had turned even at six-thirty in the morning
and it was a strange but exhilarating feeling and so
out of Bella's experience that she finally understood
why people drove hotted-up cars.

She noticed Scott's new Volvo was already parked
outside. 'Boring car,' she muttered, and then laughed
at herself. Before she'd locked the car behind her
Scott had arrived, with a scowl on his face.

Bella refused to be cowed by his grumpy look and
concentrated on why she was here. They must have
had another birth so the day would be a busy one.

He met her on the kerb. 'Why are you driving his
car?'

Bella raised her chin. She had finished with being
browbeaten by anyone. 'Need a bit more sleep do
you, Scott?' Bella asked sweetly.

Scott stopped and tilted his head. An unwilling
smile touched his lips and he rubbed the bristles on
his chin. 'Maybe.'

Bella could feel the shift in their relationship and

his acceptance of her mild criticism. Actually, it was pleasant to have a bit of fun with Scott. 'Light' was a good way to keep their relationship 'distant'. Fun was something she hadn't ever associated with their past—intensity, awareness, frustration and embarrassment had all been there in spades, but never fun. Maybe her outburst yesterday had cleared the air a little.

She mentally shrugged. 'I'd better go in. Night staff will be glad to go home if they've had another busy night.'

Scott nodded and the smile was still in his voice. 'I'll do the ward round later. Maybe I'll be more civil.'

'Sounds good.' Bella carried on towards the steps and Scott watched her walk away.

Scott decided Bella had taken his initial shock at seeing her in that boy's car and flipped it back on him, and he'd deserved it.

The new Bella would take some getting used to but he had a feeling the journey could be worth the bumps in the road. Maybe he had been insufferable over the last month. He wasn't usually a moody person but the last week had played havoc with his mind.

Self-analysis hadn't really been his forte but Bella's home truths just kept coming. He sighed and headed for his car but he couldn't help the curl of his lip as he looked at that boy's vehicle. '"Bite Me",' he huffed as he climbed into the Volvo. He still wanted to know why she was driving that car.

When Scott came back for the ward round, Bella was buried in her office with a mountain of paperwork and he stood at the door for a few heartbeats and watched her. Her head was down and a tiny frown creased her forehead.

How could he not have seen she'd changed? Probably grown more than he had. Mentally he sighed. He coughed and she looked up. She smiled at him but the smile was distracted.

'You're back.' She stated the obvious and he raised his eyebrows.

'Funny, that.'

Bella ignored his comment and stood up. 'Abbey's ready to go this morning, and Melissa's Tina has had three bradycardias since I've been here. She's self-stimulating but we're keeping her on the monitor for the rest of the day.'

He nodded. It wasn't uncommon for premature babies to have runs of slower heartbeats every now and then, especially after feeds. 'Sounds sensible. As long as she's reverting back to normal rate on her own then I'm sure Tina will be fine. She'll grow out of it,' Scott reinforced Bella's thoughts as he followed her down the corridor.

They entered the first room and Rohan was cooing at his son while Abbey put the last of her pyjamas in a suitcase on the bed.

'Finally get to take your family home with you, Rohan.' Scott smiled at his partner and winked at Abbey. 'He's been like a cat on a hot tin roof, waiting for today, and cancelled a whole morning's appointments to take you home.' He concentrated on Abbey. 'How are you and Lachlan?'

Abbey smiled serenely down at her baby. 'I'm well and young Lachlan has moments of unusual interest—but I'm getting the hang of him. It's certainly easier showing others what to do than mastering it myself.'

They all laughed and Bella handed Scott the infant stethoscope to perform Lachlan's discharge check. Rohan laid his son carefully down in the cot and Scott undid the baby's little jacket to listen to his heart and check his hips. When he'd finished the examination he straightened and ticked off the sections in the new-born health record.

'What do you think of Bella's new car, Scott?' Rohan's intention of teasing Bella fell flat when Scott stunned them all with his vehemence.

'I think she's irresponsible for driving it and it's probably a death trap.'

Jaws dropped around the room and Bella could have kicked both men for ruining the happy going-home mood for Abbey. She brushed past the awkwardness in her quiet voice.

'Don't take any notice of Scott, he needs another few hours' sleep and a reality check.' She smiled at her brother-in-law. 'The car's great to drive and if Blake leaves I may have to buy it off him.'

'Like hell,' Scott muttered, and Bella met her sister's startled eyes across the bed.

What's with him? Abbey seemed to be asking.

Bella mouthed, 'Later,' and everyone pretended that Scott hadn't said anything unusual.

Rohan's eyebrows had nearly disappeared into his hairline. He seemed determined to keep putting his foot in it. 'I met young Blake over the fence this morning. He's a bit of a card.' Scott glanced without expression at Rohan who raised his eyebrows. 'I've always wanted a scorpion tattoo.'

Abbey laughed and said, 'I can just see it.'

The general amusement that followed lightened the tension. The rest of Scott's visit scraped through as customary.

Bella practically dragged him into the next room where he seemed to have regained his equanimity for his next patient. By the end of the round things appeared normal on the surface and Bella was glad to push him out of the door.

When he'd left, Bella headed back to Abbey's room to see if her sister needed anything before her discharge. She paused at the door and the thought hit her that it was a strange thing to see Abbey as a baby's mother.

Even more strange to see her big sister a little unsure of herself when her years of experience should have given her more knowledge and confidence than any other new mother.

But Bella could see it didn't work that way and it was a light-bulb moment. Maybe Abbey wasn't as infallible as Bella had always assumed she was?

Abbey looked up and smiled and Bella moved into the room. Her brother-in-law left to carry his wife's suitcase to the car and as soon as he was out of earshot Abbey said, 'So, what's going on between you and Scott?'

'Apart from the fact that he's tired and irritable today?' Bella shrugged. 'He came around on Friday and Saturday nights for the bus run and he's been different ever since.'

'How do you feel about that?' Abbey looked at her

sister with some concern, last year's attack on both their minds.

'Better than I would have a year ago, but probably because I've got my confidence back. It will be a relief not to tread so lightly around him. Maybe we can get along better now.'

Abbey bit her lip and nodded but her silence spoke volumes. Bella met her eyes. 'I'm not interested in a relationship with Scott so don't look at me that way.'

'He's hurt you once,' was all Abbey had time to say before Rohan came back into the room and the conversation stopped.

'Scott's got a bee in his bonnet today,' Rohan said. 'When I heard you had a young man move into the house I thought it was a good thing. I don't think my partner agrees.'

'Scott has old-fashioned ideas.' Bella shrugged.

'What's Scott's problem with this young bloke? The guy's got good taste in cars.' Rohan was more interested in Blake's car if truth be told. 'I used to lust after an SLR when I was a teenager.' He glanced at his wife. 'When I was young and single.'

'Ha!' Abbey threw a look over her shoulder while she dressed Lachlan in his going-home clothes. 'You were single but never lived until you came to an exciting town like Gladstone.'

'It's the scenery I like around here.' Rohan nodded judiciously. 'And the beautiful women.' He swooped and kissed his wife.

Abbey laughed and rested back in his arms. 'I think you need to go home with your son.'

'And my wife.' He kissed her again and they both laughed as Bella slipped from the room. They were like newly-weds, Bella thought. For some people, marriage was the answer, but she liked her new-found self-sufficiency and the fact that she only had to please herself. That way she couldn't get hurt.

When Bella arrived home that night, Blake was peeling potatoes in the kitchen for Vivie. Vivie was laughing and young Ro was cruising the furniture on wobbly legs, looking for something to put in his mouth. It was a very domestic picture and Bella had to smile.

'So, what have you guys been up to today?' Bella asked as she pilfered a carrot stick off the pile.

Vivie grinned and then swooped to pick up her son and drag Bella from the room. 'Come and see. Blake fixed one of the chairs in the study.' Bella followed Vivie into the study and Blake leant on the door and watched them.

Bella sat experimentally on the seat edge of the stuffed chair. Instead of sinking into it, the chair was surprisingly firm and very comfortable.

'That's great, Blake. How did you do that?' Bella bounced a couple of times to experiment.

'I just added a board underneath and repacked the wadding. I'll do the other one tomorrow.' Blake grinned. 'Hope you didn't mind but it was pretty crook.'

Bella laughed. 'I don't mind at all. And I had fun driving your car.'

Blake coughed. 'Driving to work isn't fun. You should take it for a real run—go out to South West Rocks or down to Port Macquarie. There's a one-hundred-and-ten zone just past Port. Get it on the highway and really wind it out.'

Bella couldn't quite see herself cramped by the speed limit. 'Thank you for the offer. I might just do that one day.' They all trooped back into the kitchen. 'Aunt Sophie and I are going next door to see Abbey in a minute so if you're looking for me that's where I'll be.'

Abbey's house already had a visitor. All day at work Scott had thought about Rohan and Abbey, happy with their new family, enjoying all the things he'd never had. Not as a dog in the manger, more as a need to see what it could have been like if his wife had included him in the news of his son's birth. But even in the early days of his marriage he'd never had that rapport with his ex-wife that flowed between his two closest friends.

Although Scott had only intended a brief drop-in, Rohan had pressed him to stay and they had just finished the late afternoon tea the proud father had prepared.

Abbey stood up to answer her baby's cry from the bedroom. 'I'll leave you boys. My new master is calling and I want to change him before Aunt Sophie comes across.'

Scott stood as well. 'If you're having visitors, I'll go, too.'

Rohan waved him back into his seat. 'Sit for a minute. I want to talk to you.'

Scott eyed his friend warily as he sank back into his chair. 'That sounds ominous.'

'Not ominous. Concerned.' Rohan shrugged. 'My life's changed a lot in the year since I met Abbey. I have you to thank for that when I agreed to locum for you. I'm returning the favour.'

'Don't mention it.' Scott tried to divert his friend but Rohan was determined to say his piece.

'I had no idea that marriage and a family could be like this.' Rohan spread his arms to encompass the whole house. 'Every day is a diamond.' He shrugged, slightly embarrassed by his eloquence. 'And I think you should take the time to smell the roses, too.'

'Oh, I can smell them—' Scott's cynicism was clear '—but it's a bit late for me. Besides, I don't have time.'

Rohan shook his head. 'There's more to life than being on call for the town. I remember in med school, after that woman you married left, you were good fun and drove a car not unlike the one next door you seem to hate so much. I haven't seen that side of you since I moved here. You need to raise expectations of your life goals to include family and marriage again. Start having fun. In the last year I can't remember you socialising with anyone except us,' Rohan said.

'Can I go now?' Scott stood up and his friend rose, too.

'Yes, you can go.' Rohan looked at his partner under his brows. 'And stop picking on Bella.'

At that, Scott laughed. 'Have you listened to Bella lately? I think she could chew me up and spit me out.' He smiled at Rohan and held out his hand. 'Sorry I was short. I appreciate your concern, you're a good friend and I hear what you're saying.'

Rohan clapped him on the back. 'Lecture endeth.'

'Glad to hear it. Now I'm out of here before Sophie

comes and tells me I'm going bald or my ears need cleaning, or worse.'

Rohan grinned. 'She must really like you. She never says that to me.' He glanced out the door. 'Too late anyway.'

Rohan turned towards the window and, sure enough, Bella and her aunt had almost reached the back door.

'You'll pay if she hassles me,' Scott said in an undertone, but his eyes were really on Bella. He didn't see Rohan bite his lip to hide his smile as he strode to the back door to open it for his aunt-in-law.

'Welcome, Sophie. Abbey's gone to dress Lachlan for your arrival,' Rohan said.

'Well, I haven't dressed up for his arrival.' Sophie glanced down at her lounge dress, the like of which she wore most days. Then she looked at Scott. 'But Dr Rainford didn't iron his shirt so I feel better now.'

Scott met Rohan's laughing eyes and as if to say, What did I tell you? 'Hello, Sophie, it's always nice to see you,' Scott said as he offered her his chair.

Sophie snorted. 'I'll bet.' She waved him away. 'I'm not sitting. I'll go and find my great-nephew.' She glanced at her niece who'd been silent beside her. 'Are you coming or staying with them, Bella?'

'I'll follow in a minute.' Bella shook her head and Scott couldn't take his eyes off her hair as it floated in a crinkled cloud over her shoulders. It was so rare that he saw Bella's red hair loose that she'd caught him unprepared. Suddenly what Rohan had said was all the more relevant. He was letting his life go by.

Bella was not some eighteen-year-old girl who hadn't seen the world. She was a flesh-and-blood woman that he'd given up for her own good. Maybe it was time to start afresh and see where it led.

'So, what are you fellows doing?' Bella seemed oblivious to Scott's scrutiny and Rohan clapped her on the shoulder.

'I'm off to hear Sophie's verdict on Lachlan and Scott's been here to sample my cooking. I made pancakes for afternoon tea.' Rohan preened.

'What a model husband,' Bella teased, and Scott watched her gaze follow Rohan out of the room. When she turned back to look at him her eyes widened.

'What?' she said, and brushed her nose. 'Have I got a spot on my face or something?'

Scott shook his head. The idea he'd had last night didn't seem so crazy today. 'You look incredibly beautiful with your hair down. You should wear it like that more often.' He met her eyes. 'Do you have to stay here with your aunt or can you come and see something I'd like to show you?'

Bella tilted her head. 'I'm sure Rohan can get Aunt Sophie safely across the yard. I'll just let them know. Will it take long?'

'Does it matter?'

He could tell she was puzzled by his persistence and not sure how to read the situation. There was nothing threatening in his suggestion. It was a little odd perhaps, but he could tell she was intrigued.

'I suppose not. Won't be a minute, then.' She left the room to find her aunt, and Scott stared thoughtfully after her.

He'd had the idea last night but had shied away from offering Bella something so personal. He still couldn't imagine Bella being a big part of his life. What had he to offer her that was different to twelve years ago? A twenty-year-old son? The bitterness twisted his stomach. She was vibrant and beautiful and full of life. The trouble was, when she looked as amazing as she did today he couldn't help trying. Rohan was right. He needed to take a few chances with his life or he might just be left with more regrets.

When Bella came back, Scott was at his most inscrutable. Bella kept looking sideways at him as they crossed the lawn to his car. 'Do you want me to take Blake's car,' she said, 'so you don't have to run me home?'

Scott gave her one of his 'spare me' looks. 'I'd be happy if you never took Blake's car again. In fact…' He stopped. 'Why are you driving that boy's car?'

Bella shrugged. 'Because mine died.'

Scott's frown lightened. 'Why didn't you tell me? I could get my garage to pick it up for you. I'm sure they'll have it going in no time.'

'No, you won't.' Bella stopped and turned to face him. 'Did I miss something here? Why do you suddenly think you can run my life?'

Scott winced. He'd spoken without thinking. The fact was, he really hated the thought of Bella's easy relationship with her new boarder. He didn't even want to think about the fact that there was less of an age difference between Blake and Bella than there was between himself and Bella. The green-eyed monster was going to get him into big trouble if he wasn't careful. 'I meant, if you'd like, I could get them to come for your car.'

Bella narrowed her eyes, and he could see she was only slightly mollified.

'There's no need. Blake says he'll have it fixed by the day after tomorrow.'

Scott swallowed the acid in his mouth at that statement and wisely held his peace. 'Fine. I would still like to show you something, though, if you'll come.'

Reluctantly Bella started towards his car again. 'So, what is it that you want to show me and where is it?'

He opened her door for her and the conversation halted as he walked around and climbed into the driver's seat. Scott didn't answer as he started the engine and put the car into gear. He hoped she wouldn't tell him to stop when she found out.

'Just to my place,' he said casually. 'What I want to show you is on the side verandah.' He'd felt her stiffen beside him when he'd mentioned his house but, as he'd hoped, the mention of the verandah drew Bella's thoughts away from the fact that they'd be alone in his house for the first time in too many years.

He'd read her thoughts correctly because she looked out of the window to avoid his eyes and said, 'Your house didn't have a verandah, but it's been a long time since I've been there.'

He couldn't help the picture in his mind. All those years ago Bella had come and blushingly offered him her heart. He'd never forget the pain in her face when he'd said he didn't return her feelings and never would. Luckily, she hadn't seen the pain in his as she'd walked away that afternoon.

'The house has changed,' Scott said as he forced his thoughts back to the present. 'I've had the verandahs added and the landscapers in. I think you'll notice a difference.'

It wasn't so much a difference, Bella thought ten minutes later, as a complete transformation.

The older cottage had been expanded to include the huge four-sided verandahs and a spacious loft that took advantage of the rural views and those onto the river.

Downstairs, it was the individual pieces of woodwork that drew her attention. The television was housed in a lowboy-type cabinet with clubbed feet and different types of wood inlaid across the doors. She walked across and ran her hand down a panel.

'I've never seen this type of pattern before.' She glanced around and there were occasional tables and a desk in the same design. 'It's beautiful.' She stroked the arm of a rocking chair obviously made by the same carpenter and then curled up in it to try it out. 'I love the strength and adaptability of wood.'

'I'm glad,' was all he said, and he held his hand out to help her up. 'Come and see outside.' She didn't want to touch him, was afraid to, but was trapped into taking his hand briefly until she'd found her feet. She disengaged her fingers quickly and Scott smiled at her strangely and followed her out onto the verandah.

The back yard had been converted to a miniature rain-forest hideaway with a tiny rock-lined swimming pool and spa reached by a Japanese-style curved bridge that led off the verandah.

'Love the bridge.' Bella couldn't help herself as she ran her fingers along the wooden rail.

'I'm pleased how it turned out.' Scott stroked the

curve in the wood. 'I'd never done anything like it before.'

Bella turned slowly towards him. 'Did you make the bridge? And the rest of the furniture?'

Scott nodded and shrugged. 'Yes, I've been doing it for about twelve years, but that's not what I wanted to show you.'

Bella couldn't believe it. It was like she hadn't known him at all. There was this secret side of him that nobody talked about—or at least nobody talked about to her. Bella shook her head and followed him along the verandah.

Scott led the way around the side of the house and then he stopped in front of the most beautiful piece of furniture Bella had ever seen.

It was polished rosewood, a magnificently carved chaise longue. 'This was one of the first things I made. Do you like it?' His voice lacked his usual assurance and Bella glanced at him and then back at his work.

The chaise stood on an ancient and slightly moth-eaten Persian carpet that glowed with colour and reflected the pinkish hue of the wood so that the seat seemed to float above the floor.

'Like it? It's one of the most glorious pieces of furniture I've ever seen. But why did you want me to see it now?'

'Because I want you to have it.' Bella shook her head instinctively and Scott stepped closer. 'Because you said that Rohan took the one in your study. I don't use it and I'd like you to have it. To tell the truth, it was actually inspired by Abbey's old chaise a long time ago.'

His words shifted the mood in the room and Bella took one step backwards to distance herself.

Scott could see she was uncomfortable and he strove to lighten the mood. 'Besides, I can't stand the thought of sitting on that uncomfortable chair you have.'

'Blake fixed it.' As soon as the words were out of her mouth she regretted them. Scott's face hardened and he turned away. 'Fine. It was just an idea.'

Bella felt terrible. 'It's not fine.' She stepped up to him and rested her hand gently on her shoulder. He flinched under the light pressure and she couldn't help the soothing stroke that followed. 'I'm sorry, Scott.' She was unaware that she stroked him again. 'It's just that you took me by surprise and it's a gift of such magnitude I'd feel in your debt. And I don't like that feeling. I don't ever want to be in anyone's power again.'

Finally she felt him loosen under her hand. He turned slowly to face her and his expression was, as usual, difficult to read.

'I don't want you in my power, Bella. I do care for you and it would give me pleasure for you to have the chaise, but I can understand your reluctance. Let's forget I ever offered it. Come and see the garden while you're here.' He held out his hand.

She couldn't turn down that offer, too, so tentatively Bella put her hand in his. His fingers held hers gently and the warmth from his touch made the swirling in her stomach start again.

Unconsciously, she paused in her stride at the implications of her reaction to him. If she didn't care about him, why was she affected by the feel of her hand in his? Scott pulled on her arm gently and she flicked a glance up at his face. He was smiling and there was nothing but friendship for her to see. She kick-started her legs and walked down the steps with him onto the lawn below.

'It looks like a magazine garden. You must have a green thumb to keep all this alive.' Bella strove to keep her voice normal despite the tumultuous feelings just holding his hand was doing to her stomach and, further along, her legs.

Scott laughed with genuine amusement and Bella felt some of her tension seep away with the pleasant sound. 'The gardener has a green thumb. Mine's wood-coloured, but I do enjoy the way he can make it all flourish.'

Bella smiled back as they wandered down a winding path to a small fountain. 'I know what you mean. Vivie has the most fabulous herb garden and every time I look after it something seems to die.'

They stopped at the fountain and Bella could see golden fish swimming through the underwater greenery. She turned back towards the house. 'It's magical here, Scott. You must be very proud.'

He shrugged. 'The magic is in the person I'm showing it to.' Bella shot him a look and he shrugged without explaining, but the awareness was there again between them. 'Come on, I'll take you home.'

That was what she wanted, Bella told herself as they turned back to the house but she was walking more slowly. Bella thought about all the hours Scott must have spent carving the design on the chaise longue and why he'd want to give such a labour-intensive piece to her. Then she wondered exactly how long ago he had made it if it was the first thing he'd made. 'Can I see where you do all your carpentry before I go?'

Bella didn't know where the words came from but they had the subconsciously desired effect.

CHAPTER FIVE

'IF YOU wish,' Scott said, and Bella nodded her head.

This was not a good idea, Scott thought, but he couldn't resist the temptation to keep Bella with him for even a few minutes longer. Seeing her drift around his house, her fingers trailing across his possessions like he'd once dreamed about, was too powerful a drug.

He turned off the path underneath a huge leopard tree and towards a building set on the edge of the property and the tension built in his shoulders. There had been a lot of emotions in that shed. It was his sanctuary and no one had been in it for many years. He ran his hand along a high ledge and produced the key to open the door. Then stood back to allow Bella to enter. He watched her enter like a watchful gazelle, sniffing the air and eyes darting for hidden dangers but filled with curiosity now she'd decide to take the risk.

All Bella's senses were on full alert as she entered the room.

The room was cool, soundproof and very tidy, but the smell of wood shavings and the lingering tang of varnish hung enticingly in the air.

She glanced around. 'Do you work in here often?'

His face shuttered. 'Nearly every day this week. When I need tranquillity. A problem that needs a solution, a sad birth.' He shrugged. 'The wood helps my thought processes.'

A cane basket sat in the corner on the floor almost overflowing with wood sweepings, and Bella walked across and picked up one particularly long and curly shaving. She closed her eyes and breathed in the scent of freshly cut timber and then hung it in her hair above her eyes. '"There was a girl who had a little curl, right in the middle of her forehead."'

Scott leaned back against the door and completed the verse. '"And when she was good, she was very, very good, and when she was bad she was horrid."'

'So what am I, Scott?' Bella couldn't help the slip into danger. 'Good or horrid?'

'Definitely horrid.' Scott crossed the room and stopped in front of her. He plucked the shaving from her hair. Their eyes met and time stopped for several seconds as they both thought of the kiss the other night. Scott said, 'Horrid but infinitely kissable.'

Bella blinked but didn't have much time for evasive action as Scott closed the distance between them and captured her lips with his. His arms came around her and he gathered her close into his warmth. Yet she knew his hold was loose enough for her to escape if she wanted to.

Bella planned to step back but somehow it never happened. The taste of Scott's mouth against hers meshed with the smells and coolness of the workshop. When he pulled her more firmly against the hardness of his chest that feeling blended with the masculinity of the environment and filled her brain with wicked mind pictures of woodshavings and strong benches.

She couldn't do anything but kiss him back and it was addictively delicious. Her fingers reached up and sank into his hair and his hands slid down and cupped her buttocks until she was on tiptoe, straining to stay attached to the floor. The kiss went on and on and suddenly the fire they'd ignited threatened to consume them both and Scott groaned as he lifted his mouth slowly and lingeringly from hers and set her down.

They stared at each other and both tried to steady their breathing. 'I get very passionate about my wood-work,' he said, and Bella nodded.

'It's passionate stuff.' Her voice was higher-pitched than normal and she cleared her throat as they both stepped apart. 'I think I should go home now.'

Scott nodded and gestured for her to precede him from the room. She waited while he locked the door and then headed for the house. She could feel his eyes on her neck the whole way and her face flamed as she remembered the way she'd ground herself against him—and how that had made her feel. Once they were inside the house, Scott still didn't say anything as he picked his keys up from the hall table.

Bella didn't know whether it was a good thing they weren't talking about what just happened or a bad idea. At his continued silence she started to worry. Was he going to pretend it had never happened? Or was he going to assume that any time he wanted to kiss her she'd be happy with that? Bella squirmed. It had only been that wonderful smell of carpentry that had brought out the wanton in her.

Finally the silence got to her. Honestly, she thought, he was a doctor, you'd imagine he'd be skilled at putting people at ease. 'I don't think much of your bedside manner, Dr Rainford.'

Scott glanced across at Bella and almost pulled the car over to kiss her again. She was flushed and he could see she was embarrassed and she probably wanted to tear his eyes out. He hadn't spoken because he didn't know what to say. He'd almost pulled her down on the floor of the shed and lost himself in her and she'd have been helpless to stop him because they'd both been blind to reason. Didn't she realise that?

'There's nothing wrong with my bedside manner.' The sex maniac inside his head whispered, When I put a couch in the workshop I'll show you. He almost groaned at the picture that painted.

She folded her arms across her chest and stared out through the windscreen. She probably thought he was insufferable. Scott suppressed a smile. When the car pulled up outside her house, without looking at him, she said, 'Thank you for bringing me home.'

Before she could pull the handle he said, 'Stay there, I'll open your door.' He could tell she fumed as she waited. She probably wasn't sure whether she was more angry at him for telling her what to do or at herself for doing what she was told. He hid another smile and opened her door.

She climbed out as if the hordes were after her. Scott just stood there as Bella muttered, 'Thank you.' And marched up the front path. Scott wasn't sure if he'd advanced his suit or killed it.

Tuesday

The next morning Bella had decided to ignore the events of yesterday. The kiss had definitely been down to proximity, that and the ghosts of twelve years ago in Scott's house which had still been at the back of her mind. The fact that their kiss had transported her to a place she'd felt inclined to linger in she didn't want to think about.

Bella tugged the brush through her hair in punishing strokes. She wasn't the naïve girl from the past— the one awed by a handsome young doctor who'd seemed to understand everything about her.

The Scott of today didn't understand her at all and she didn't want him to.

When Bella went downstairs, Blake had Vivie's baby, Ro, on his lap and both Vivie and the baby were laughing. Blake looked up when Bella entered.

He grinned and bounced young Ro on his lap. 'Your car won't be ready till Monday because we're waiting for a part for the engine.'

Bella poured the cereal into her bowl and nodded. 'Monday's fine. I can take the bus if you need your car. I never thought mine would ever go again.'

Blake rolled his eyes. 'Take my car, please. That bus is embarrassing.'

Bella grinned and finished her breakfast. 'You're a vehicle snob, that's what you are.'

Fifteen minutes later she parked Blake's car outside Maternity and she smiled as the engine gurgled its way to silence. Her brother-in-law's car was here so he must have been on call.

Rohan was at the desk when she went in and he winked when he saw her.

'Hi, Bella. So, where did you get to yesterday with Scott?'

Bella looked around at the interested faces at the desk and raised her eyebrows. 'Is this start-a-rumour day, Rohan?'

Rohan didn't even have the grace to look a little guilty as he realised how his statement must have sounded.

'Oops,' he said with a wicked smile, and left.

Bella sighed as she sat down.

Sharon, despite her eagerness to get home after the night shift, leaned towards Bella and pretended to elbow her. 'And what was that all about, boss?'

Sharon and Bella had been in the same class at school and Bella knew she wasn't going to get away without replying.

'Scott showed me a piece of furniture he'd made, and the rest was Rohan's imagination.' She looked at Sharon. 'Did you know that Scott was a carpenter?'

Sharon nodded. 'He gave Abbey a beautiful round table to auction the year before last when we wanted to raise money for the ward.' She smiled at the memory. 'Half the women in the hospital bid for it but I think it went to some rich widow who fancied him. It didn't do her any good. The money bought a new Sonicaid.'

'Oh,' said Bella. 'Abbey didn't mention it.'

Sharon shrugged. 'It was before you came back from Sydney.'

Bella pushed away the thought that Abbey hadn't talked voluntarily about Scott to her for many years. She nodded and sat further back in her chair.

'So, what happened on the ward through the

night?' Sharon shot a quick look at Bella and then shrugged as if to say, Was that it?

Bella raised her eyebrows and waited and Sharon grinned. She started the handover report.

An hour later, Bella had had time to speak to all the patients and was back at the desk. Scott strolled in and Bella tried to think cool thoughts to stop the blush that she could feel in her cheeks.

'It's warm this morning,' Scott said with a saintly smile, and Bella narrowed her eyes.

'So it seems,' she said with restraint. She didn't look at him again as she moved off down the hall with the patient files and Scott had to follow.

In the first room, Melissa's baby was in her mother's arms. 'Tina seems to have stopped her bradycardias,' Bella said.

Scott cupped the baby's foot in his big hand and the sight pulled strangely at Bella's stomach. She was noticing more and more about him every day and she couldn't seem to stop herself.

'That must make you feel better, Melissa.' Scott smiled at the girl.

Melissa smiled back. 'Yep. When I heard the machine noises slow down I could feel my own heart go faster. It was pretty scary. Are you sure she shouldn't have the machine when I go home?'

Scott nodded. 'Yes. I'm sure.' He sat on the edge of the bed. 'Tina's bradycardias don't change her skin colour so even though her heart rate and breathing slows down her breathing doesn't stop. She's still getting all the oxygen she needs. You'll find that any bradycardias that she has now will usually be after a feed and she will have fewer and fewer of them as she grows. I would be very surprised if she was still having any by the time she's ready to go home.' He smiled sympathetically. 'You need to get used to the idea there won't be a machine to listen to her all the time, but I know it's hard.'

Melissa nodded and glanced ruefully at Bella. 'That's pretty much what Bella said.'

Scott looked across at Bella and his face was dead-pan. 'Sister Wilson and I agree on everything.'

Bella nodded, and refused to dispute anything that would undermine Melissa's belief in Scott's words.

When Scott looked a little disappointed by her lack of dissension, Bella had to suppress her smile. He looked back at Melissa. 'How's Tina with her feeds?'

Melissa shrugged. 'I can't get her to feed from me but she'll take my milk from a bottle every second feed. Bella says that's pretty good for her prematurity.'

'My word, it is.' Scott nodded and glanced at the feed chart. 'And how are you after the birth?'

The girl shrugged. 'I don't even feel like I had a baby. I can't wait to take her home but I know I have to be patient.'

'It's tough,' Scott agreed, 'but you're doing a great job.' He stood up. 'I'll see you tomorrow.'

They left Melissa and the rest of the round was accomplished swiftly.

Back at the desk, Scott couldn't resist commenting, 'I see you're still driving the hot rod.'

Bella nodded. 'Mine won't be ready till Monday and it's more fun than the bus.'

Scott's lip curled. 'It's a death trap.'

Bella shook her head. 'Now I'll have to disagree

with the great Dr Rainford there, which is strange
when we agree on everything.' Bella shrugged. 'In
fact, I'm planning on taking it for a spin this afternoon
down to Port Macquarie. Just to open it up on the
highway.'

Bella had no intention of doing anything of the
kind but Scott's persistent ridicule of Blake's car annoyed her.

Scott was silent for a minute and Bella waited to
hear what disparaging comment he'd make now.
'Want a passenger?' Scott's question hung in the air
between them and Bella froze. Her mind blanked and
she had a horrible feeling her mouth was open.

'Well?' There was an underlying amusement in his
persistence as he pressured her, almost as if he knew
she'd never meant to do it.

'Sure! Why not?' Bella threw back at him reck-
lessly, and they stared at each other, each daring the
other to back down. In the end Scott nodded and
headed for the exit.

'Better bring a spare pair of underpants,' Bella muttered.

Scott froze on his way to the door and looked back
at Bella incredulously. '*What* did you say?'

Bella looked up innocently. 'I said I'd better check
the spare on the off chance.' Scott didn't look convinced and Bella glanced with pretended nonchalance
at the clock on the wall. 'I'll pick you up at six. That
will give us almost two hours of light with daylight
saving. Unless you want to change your mind?' She
showed her teeth.

Scott bared his right back. 'I'll be ready.'

When Scott had gone across to the other side of

the hospital to see his patients in Children's Ward, Bella sank into the chair and put her head in her hands. What had she done?

She had little time to worry about it. The day nurse, Michelle, had just made them coffee when Bella heard the front door open. She walked out to see who it was and her heart plummeted.

A terrified young mother rushed up to Bella and thrust her limp baby into her arms. The baby was blue and lifeless. 'She stopped breathing. She's sick. Get the doctor.'

'Michelle!' Bella's call had Michelle on her heels as she ran to the nursery with the baby in her arms. Bella hit her fist against the raised red cardiac-arrest button on her way to the infant resuscitation trolley, and the reassuring beep echoed through the corridors. Help would be here soon. Bella squeezed back the panic in her throat and concentrated. 'Airway. Cardiac output,' she said under her breath.

She placed the baby's head towards her on the trolley, in the 'sniffing' position, but couldn't see any reason for the baby not to be breathing. Quickly she tried to hear a heartbeat with the stethoscope but couldn't find one.

The baby's mother was crying and wringing her hands and Bella glanced briefly at her. 'Did you find her like this or did she stop breathing on the way here?'

'She wasn't breathing when I found her in her crib but she started again when I picked her up. Then she stopped again on the way here.'

'That's great. You did the right thing. Help is on the way,' Bella said as she twisted the knob to send oxygen surging through the mask of the resuscitation bag. She held it over the baby's face and gave three quick puffs of the clear bag, watching the infant's lungs inflate and deflate. So there was no obstruction.

Michelle came to a hurried stop beside her and Bella handed her the bag. 'Grab this and bag her, please. I can't find a pulse and we'll do ECM until help arrives.'

The next two minutes felt like a lifetime and although the baby didn't breathe, her colour improved and Bella thought she heard a tiny thready beat when she stopped after the second two minutes.

Scott skidded into the room and Bella had never been more pleased to see him. Two younger doctors from the emergency department followed him in, and if the situation hadn't been so grave Bella would have laughed at how out of breath they were compared to the older doctor.

She gave verbal handover to Scott. 'Mum found her limp in bed. Baby started to breathe when picked up and stopped again on the way to hospital. Limp and blue on arrival and I couldn't hear a heartbeat. Think there's one now, though.'

'Good stuff.' His face was intense as he examined the infant.

Bella continued with the ECM except when Scott listened to the baby's heartbeat.

'She's got a good heart rate now.' Bella changed places with Michelle when Scott indicated she could stop cardiac massage and Michelle drew the mother to a chair to sit down.

'Close. Very close.' They put a head box with oxygen around the baby's head and watched her. 'We'll put an IV in and get her hooked up to the monitors, then transfer her to Port Macquarie so the paediatricians can give her a thorough going over.'

He glanced at the mother and lowered his voice. 'I'd say this was a too-close-for-comfort, sudden-infant-death-syndrome scenario. They may never find out why her baby did this, the poor woman.'

Bella nodded and she could feel the sting of tears in her own eyes. She couldn't imagine anything more frightening than the thought of losing a child. She wanted to hug the young mother but Michelle was doing that so Bella smiled mistily at Scott instead.

Scott stayed while they waited for the ambulance to transport mother and baby to the larger base hospital. One of the emergency doctors was going with them just in case.

Scott reassured the mother before she left. 'Because she's been so stable since she's woken up, it does look better for her. The paediatricians will look after you both.'

Bella hugged the woman. 'Take care.'

'Thank you.' She brushed away her tears. 'I'll come and see you when we get out of hospital.'

'I'd like that,' Bella said, and she stood beside Scott as the ambulance drove away. Bella wanted to cry to relieve the tension but she fought it. As if he sensed how she was feeling, Scott rested his hand on her shoulder and leaned his forehead against hers. It felt so comforting Bella wanted to stay there all day.

'Good job, Bella,' he said, and she felt the tears prick her eyes again.

'I was very glad to see you,' she said in a shaky voice, and he smiled as she stepped away.

'That's what I like to hear.' He tilted his head at her. 'Make sure you're glad to see me at six o'clock. That's if you still want to get out this evening?'

Not surprisingly Bella had forgotten about their plans for Blake's car. The thought of wind in her hair and being right away from the hospital sounded good.

'I'm no piker,' she said bravely, and turned back into the nursery to help Michelle clean up.

At six o'clock Bella's misgivings had returned and multiplied ten times. Blake had thought it a great idea for Bella to go for a 'decent spin', as he called it, but he'd looked at her strangely when she'd mentioned she was taking Scott.

'I think it will be good company for Bella to take Dr Rainford,' Vivie said, and Bella smiled weakly back.

'Thanks, Vivie.' She glanced at the clock again. 'Could you leave my dinner in the fridge, please? I'll reheat it when I come home.'

'Sure.' Vivie tilted her head knowingly. 'If you've already eaten, I'm sure we can find another hungry person to feed it to.'

Blake looked up, not unlike a starving puppy, and both women laughed. Bella jingled the keys and waved on her way out.

Scott was standing on his front verandah with a small basket when she pulled up. Bella leaned across the seats and pushed opened his door.

He climbed in. 'Thank you,' he said.

'I wasn't being polite.' Bella grinned. 'That door doesn't open from the outside.'

'Great,' Scott said, and leaned over the back to rest

the basket on the floor. 'I brought a picnic.' Then he tested that he could open the front door from the inside. 'So if we crash, the emergency services can't get in to me, is that right?'

'You're such a pessimist,' Bella said as she put the car into first gear and roared off down the street. Scott exaggerated the g-force slamback in his seat and Bella ignored him.

She'd driven with Scott before in the bus. There was no reason to feel intimidated by Scott sitting beside her now. She was a good driver and she did love the way the car cornered like it was glued to the road.

Bella double-shuffled back into second as she approached an intersection and then planted it as the lights changed to green.

Scott loosened his collar. 'Do you remember that Disney cartoon about the schizophrenic driver who changes when they get behind the wheel? Mr Walker becomes Mr Wheeler?' Scott's voice was conversational and Bella shot him a look.

'I've stayed within the speed limit.'

'Granted.' Scott's voice was dry. 'At least turn your headlights on so the other cars have more warning that you're coming.'

Bella looked over the top of her sunglasses at him as if to say, It's broad daylight. But she switched the lights on and then pushed her glasses back up her nose.

Scott ignored her sarcasm and tried some of his own. 'Can't wait for the highway.'

Bella had no intention of breaking any speed limits but he was being insufferable. She pushed in the tape deck and some high-voiced rap artist talked repetitiously with a mind-numbing bass beat in the background. She sneaked a glance at Scott's horrified face and relented, but couldn't help the giggle. 'Sorry. That time I was pulling your leg. It's not my taste either.'

'Thank God for small mercies.' Scott pretended to wipe his brow and Bella relaxed into her seat. This was fun. In fact, much of the last few days had been fun and not a little exciting. But she was too busy to worry about that now.

They left the outskirts of town and Bella sped along the highway with the windows open. The little car whipped around any slower vehicles in the overtaking lane and the roar of the wind drowned out any hope of conversation.

By the time they'd driven to the turn-off to Port Macquarie, Bella was bored with the highway. 'How about we head past Wauchope? At least I can play with the corners.'

Scott shook his head and grinned back at her. 'I have a cast-iron stomach. You won't make me carsick. Do your worst.'

Bella flicked on the indicator and they took the doughnut over the highway and sped down the tarmac towards Wauchope.

The Torana seemed to be enjoying the outing and Bella decided that she could become addicted to rally driving.

Half an hour later Scott pointed to a sign. 'I see they have a picnic area down by the river, and I brought a picnic. Let's have a break.'

Bella nodded and turned off the road. The tarmac soon disappeared and they bumped along the dirt for what seemed like miles before coming to the river. Bella pulled up in the huge deserted parking area. 'They must have been planning on a party for this place.'

Scott looked around and there was no sign of life. 'Must be an off week.' He leaned over the back and lifted the basket and waved it at her.

'Hungry?'

Bella nodded and climbed out. She found a tarpaulin in the boot to spread on the ground.

Scott planted the basket in the middle of the blue sheet and proceeded to stretch out on the ground and put his elbow over his eyes.

Bella glared at him. 'What's this?'

Scott didn't move his arm and his voice was muffled. 'Chauvinism.' Bella bit back a smile but, truth be told, she was dying of curiosity to see what was in the basket. 'Then you have to pack up afterwards.' That was all she said as she flipped off the lid.

Chicken, Camembert, avocado, what looked like shop-made potato salad, some crusty rolls and two bottles of non-alcoholic white wine. Plus a jar of sliced mango. Not a bad effort for a confirmed bachelor. 'What? No coffee?'

This time he did remove his arm but he put it back over his eyes when he saw she was joking. 'Got me,' he said.

'Well, come on, look alive. I'm starving and I want to get home not too much after dark.'

Scott sat up and edged along the tarpaulin to sit next to the basket.

While Bella made up the plates, he opened the wine

and poured it out into two plastic goblets. 'To small cars and speed limits.'

Bella grinned and took a sip. It wasn't bad. She relaxed back on her elbows and breathed in the fresh air.

'This is actually quite a radical thing to do on a weeknight,' Bella mused.

'Very,' Scott agreed, and raised his glass again for another toast. 'To radical things on weeknights,' he toasted.

They clinked plastic and both of them laughed at the dull clunky sound.

Bella stared at the clouds that were turning pink in the sunset. 'What's the most radical thing you've ever done, Scott?' The question popped out without much thought.

CHAPTER SIX

'WHAT makes you think I've ever done anything radical?' Scott stared pensively into his wine and Bella glanced across at him with a frown.

'Everyone has done something mad at least once in their life.' She smiled encouragingly and then her smile faltered. 'Tell me you have.' There was a long pause and she stifled the disappointment that accompanied the worry Scott might never have done anything remotely mad.

'You mean, apart from running off with a woman fifteen years my senior and being left soon after?' Scott watched Bella blink and for the life of him he couldn't think of anything radical he'd done since alienating Bella all those years ago. Suddenly he remembered the family planning seminar he'd been to last week. The company reps had been giving out freebies and he'd stuck a couple of condoms in his wallet to give to Rohan, along with a crack about spacing babies. 'But I don't want to talk about that radical mistake. How about something radical I have with me?' Maybe he could make her laugh.

She relaxed her shoulders as he teased her. 'But I'm not sure I want to tell you and I don't want you to get any ideas.'

Bella bristled again and he suppressed his amusement. Here with Bella, tonight, offered a precious hour of joy from nowhere, and he was savouring it.

Bella glared at him. The man was laughing at her. 'You're just saying that to whet my appetite.' His slow smile warmed that fluttery feeling back into her stomach. She took a gulp of her drink and thanked her stars that the wine wasn't potent. 'So? Give!'

He smiled again and shifted along the tarp to be closer to her. He reached into his pocket and pulled out his wallet.

Bella frowned. 'What are you doing?'

'I'm showing you something mad that I've got.'

His hands flicked open his wallet with painful slowness and slid his fingers into the back section to pull out a small package. He placed the packet in the palm of his hand. 'That's it.'

Bella peered at his hand. 'What?'

'It's a glow-in-the-dark condom.'

There was something so bizarrely out of character about Scott and his possession of a glow-in-the-dark condom that it made Bella shut her eyes and bite her lip. Serious, conservative and dignified Dr Rainford, luminescent with lust. An ordinary, flesh-coloured, non-ribbed condom discreet in his wallet perhaps, but glow-in-the-dark?

A bubble of laughter slid its way up her throat and she tried to hold it back, but the amusement escaped in a deep-throated giggle. That chuckle was followed by several more hiccups of mirth, and before she knew it Bella was rolling around on the tarpaulin, holding her stomach. Scott watched her with pretended offence until she could control herself. She lay on her back and gasped for air, holding her aching diaphragm.

Finally she managed, 'What a Boy Scout.' And wiped the tears from her eyes.

'I can see you're impressed. In fact, I've got two. I'll give you one to keep. Now, tell me about something you've done.'

Bella shook her head. 'I can't top that one.'

Scott wasn't taking that. 'It's your turn—tell me.'

Bella leaned back and stared at the darkening sky. The silence lengthened. She'd always been a wimp. 'I went topless in the hospital pool one night after lights-out.' She sighed with disgust. 'I kept my panties on because I couldn't even do the full monty.'

'That idea has potential,' he said, and glanced suggestively towards the river.

She shook her head. 'I don't think so.' Bella finished the wine in her goblet and dropped the empty cup into the picnic basket.

That fluttery feeling was coming back in her stomach and Scott's glance seemed to be getting warmer. 'Well, my compliments to the chef. It's been very pleasant, but we should go.'

Scott nodded without apparent reluctance and Bella assured herself she was glad.

'Work tomorrow,' he said. 'You have a wander down to the river and I'll do my part of the bargain and pack this away.'

Bella stood up and brushed the last crumbs from her hands. 'Thank you, kind sir.' Superfluous, she wandered down towards the rocky bank of the shallow river and stood beside a huge weeping willow with all the leaves and branches eaten off to cow-neck height. She smiled at the exactness of the bovine pruning line and turned back to the car.

Scott had folded the tarpaulin and put the basket back in the car and looked to be waiting for her to return.

'Coming,' she called as she scrambled back up the stony slope to the car. 'Do you want to drive?' she offered, but Scott shook his head with a smile.

'I like to live dangerously—you drive.'

'Well, if those are the two most radical things we've ever done, driving with me probably consti-tutes dangerous.'

He opened her door and then walked around to the passenger side to climb in. Bella leaned forward and twisted the key in the ignition, but the only response was a thready clicking noise.

Scott swivelled his head to look at Bella and folded his arms. 'I hope that wasn't what I thought it was.'

Bella glared at him and tried again. The clicking noise returned but that was it.

Bella inhaled slowly and then deliberately exhaled. 'OK, Dr Mechanic Rainford, what is that noise?'

'That, Sister Wilson, is the sound of a flat battery. Did you turn off the headlights when we stopped?'

Bella's gaze flew to the light switch and, sure enough, it was on. She switched it off hurriedly as if to make up for her lapse but, of course, it was too late. Bella slapped the steering-wheel and chewed her lip. 'You told me to turn the lights on. Why didn't you tell me to turn them off?'

Scott smiled cynically. 'A woman's logic.'

Bella glared at him and then she brightened. 'I'm a member of NRMA Road Service.'

Scott gave a half-laugh. 'Not in this car, I suspect.'

Bella frowned at him. 'Won't they come to me because I'm a member?'

Scott pulled out his mobile phone and handed it to Bella. 'Try them. But I bet you ten dollars there's no reception down in this hollow.'

Bella almost snatched the phone and punched in the six-digit number for Road Service, but the phone was dead. She passed the phone back carefully to Scott and then succumbed to an insane flurry of slapping hands on the steering-wheel again.

Scott grinned and looked away before she could see his smile.

Bella stopped, blew a strand of red hair out of her face and consciously relaxed her shoulders. Then she glared at him. 'You planned this.' Bella's accusation made Scott's eyebrows lift.

'Now, that would be radical,' he murmured, and Bella hung her head.

'I'm sorry. That was stupid. What are we going to do?'

Bella's reaction to the breakdown was strangely different to his. Scott was feeling remarkably calm and not a little pleased with the thought of spending the evening with Bella in unusual circumstances. Which was strange, as he'd normally be obsessed with being at work on time tomorrow, and available should the remote possibility arise of Rohan needing him overnight. Not to mention the fear of scandalmongers.

Scott shrugged and gestured to the darkness that was quickly falling. 'At a guess, I'd say we're going to sleep here tonight and walk to a phone in the morning.'

Scott wound his window up. 'I'd recommend winding your window up until after dusk or we'll be fodder for the mosquitoes.'

Bella hastily agreed and then she sat back in her seat and tried to think of a solution. They hadn't passed a house on the way in off the highway so that made it a couple of miles' walk at least. Then there was the dark factor.

No car was going to stop in the dark to help them anyway. She couldn't find an answer that improved on Scott's suggestion. She doubted anyone would find them or even start looking until tomorrow. Even Vivie would think she'd stayed out to tea and no one would be any wiser until she didn't turn up for work next day. She winced. The rumours would be horrendous when they did go back.

'Let's run away to Perth,' she said half-jokingly.

Scott smiled. 'Thinking about the gossips, are you?'

Bella nodded and sighed. 'Is this a radical thing to do?'

'Right up there.' His hand came across and closed over her fingers. 'It's really not a tragedy. Tomorrow morning we'll try and push the car up the slope and maybe we can clutch-start it. But it's a bit dark to do that now.'

'But when I don't turn up for work, they'll ring

Vivie and she'll ring Abbey and Rohan will ring you and you won't be home...'

'Shh.' Scott squeezed her hand and Bella could hear the thread of laughter in his voice.

'Look at it this way—we're safe, and being slightly embarrassed is nothing. As for work, I'd be a little more worried if Rohan wasn't in town, but he is. He can handle anything that needs to be handled and Sharon or whoever is on night duty will stay until you arrive.'

Bella sighed one last time and then straightened in her seat. 'You're right. I won't moan any more and I think you've been very good about this considering it was me that left the lights on.' She felt very self-righteous taking the blame and she looked across to see if Scott commended her for it.

No such luck. 'I think so, too,' he said, 'but, then, I was saving recriminations in case we got bored later.'

Bella shook her hand out of his and crossed her arms, but when she looked back he was smiling. She stared at him. Who was this man? 'You've changed so much from the grumpy shirt of last week that I barely recognise you.'

'Grumpy shirt?' he repeated wonderingly, and then became more serious. 'It's been a big week.'

They sat there for a while in surprisingly companionable silence. Then Scott leaned his head back, closed his eyes and started to talk. 'Since finding out about my son...' he grimaced '...and coming to terms with the fact that I didn't have the chance to watch a

child of mine grow up, something I would love to
have memories of, I've reassessed my life.'

She heard him sigh before he went on.

'Michael's existence and the fact that I've never
seen him has changed my perspective. It's made me
look at other areas of my life that I should have seen
to years ago.' He smiled at a memory. 'And Rohan
gave me a serve that had me thinking as well.'

Bella was intrigued. 'What did Rohan say?'

Scott opened his eyes. 'He was fairly succinct,'
Scott said wryly. 'That I need to raise expectations of
my life goals and that I can't just be there for the
town. He also said I should take time for myself and
start having fun.' He turned to look at Bella with a
grin. 'Guess we've started on the last one.'

It was dark outside the car, and a cow bellowed
not far away. Scott looked at his watch. 'It's eight-
thirty. The mosquitoes should be gone now. Do you
want to stretch your legs?' Bella nodded and Scott
opened his door.

'At least there weren't any cowpats near the car,'
Bella said brightly.

'And it's not raining, Pollyanna.' Scott was rum-
maging in the glovebox for anything else useful. 'Ta-
da.' He brandished a box of matches. 'I shall build a
campfire, and with a bit of luck someone will come
to tell us to put it out.'

'I'll help gather wood.' The idea of a campfire
shining benevolent light was very appealing and Bella
tried to remember if she'd seen any broken branches
on her short walk. It wasn't ink black yet and she
could see outlines of obstacles in front of her.

After half an hour of hard work they had a reason-able-sized firewood pile in the middle of the parking area.

Bella had brought the tarpaulin from the boot again and spread it out on the ground. The first flickers of flame seemed to spread light in gradually increasing circles and by the time the fire was well established, the whole parking area appeared friendlier. They stood together and admired Scott's handiwork.

'Well done, fire king,' Bella said. 'Now what do we do?'

Scott took Bella's hand and pulled her sideways in front of him then gently back so he could encircle her with his arms as they faced the fire. 'Are you one of these people who have to be amused all the time?'

Bella could feel the hardness of his body against her back and buttocks, and the warmth of his arms felt right, and not something she wanted to fight against.

'No,' she said in a voice half the volume of what she'd intended. She felt his chin rest gently in her hair and then the movement of his lips as he dropped a kiss on the top of her head. Bella closed her eyes. This wasn't what she'd imagined when she'd started this trip today but it felt so good she couldn't help sighing. But she needed to be careful. There was a fine line between special moments and those she'd live to regret.

They stood there for a long time and the silence between them was tranquil as they soaked up the un-expected solitude.

For Scott it was wonderful. Bella in his arms, relaxed and happy with his prowess as the fire provider, they had food and water at the river and a long night ahead to establish the beginnings of what could be the relationship he'd never allowed himself to dream of. 'Well, this is better than reruns of *Bonanza* on television,' he said with a smile in his voice.

Bella tilted her head. 'What's *Bonanza*?'

Scott shut and opened his eyes. Apart from the fact that it was an asinine thing to have said to a young and beautiful woman in his arms, her response was not surprising. She was too young to have ever seen *Bonanza* and he'd grown up with the show. What was he thinking of? He was a fool to think this relationship was going to work. His arms dropped.

'Reality check,' he murmured. 'It's an old TV show that was on before you were born.' And he walked over to throw another stick on the fire.

Bella bunched her fists against her sides. 'Now, that response was more like the angst-ridden Dr Rainford of last week,' she snapped, and Scott threw his head up and glared at her.

The words hung in the air between them. Suddenly the little picnic area wasn't as friendly any more. He took several large strides and before she knew it he was right beside her again.

He wasn't the one who was going to lose out by being with someone old and crotchety. He was trying to protect her and didn't she realise it was killing him?

'And which Dr Rainford do you prefer?' His voice was soft but that dangerous quality was back, the one from the kitchen when she'd asked about his marriage. Bella could feel the acceleration in her heart rate but she wasn't going to back down.

'I like the one in the car from an hour ago and the one from five minutes ago.'

Scott caught a thick strand of her hair between his fingers and used it to turn her head until there was barely an inch between their faces. 'What about the one in my workshop? Because I'm damned if I can get *that* Bella out of my mind.'

His lips came down on hers and Bella knew this was not a good idea, alone in the bush in the dark, and the hunger in his voice matched the hunger deep inside herself and she wanted to lean into him but she just wasn't ready for this. The warning she'd given herself was too recent.

Bella pulled away and slid out from under his arms and walked out of the circle of light towards the river.

'Where are you going?' he asked, and she turned back to look at him. The light from the fire was behind him and his face was shadowed yet surrounded by a fiery halo. He was everything she wanted in a man. It wasn't Scott she was afraid of, it was herself and the fragility of her own self-esteem if she ended in his arms tonight. She wasn't ready to risk everything she'd worked for in the last year because it felt good at the time.

'I need some space.' Time away from him to think about the ramifications of wanting to give herself to Scott and what could happen to her if he let her down again.

'Be careful,' he called after her. It was the 'be careful' that did it.

The next second her foot disappeared down a rabbit hole and her ankle twisted with excruciating sharpness as her full weight came down on it. Her cry was muffled but Scott heard it. The grass and rocks were digging into her hands as she tried to keep the weight of her body off her leg, and the tears sprang to her eyes as the burning pain shot up behind her knee. Any attempt to remove her leg from the hole made her whimper with distress.

'It's OK, sweetheart.' Scott appeared on his knees beside her and his hand ran down her calf and into the hole. 'You've jammed it good and proper and your ankle is starting to swell already. We have to get it out before it gets any fatter.'

'I do not have fat ankles.' Her voice was weak and she was trying not to cry with pain.

He patted her shoulder. 'Ankles, no, ankle, yes.'

The next few minutes were ones that Bella would have preferred to forget. When her foot finally came free, her head was swimming from the pain. Scott gathered her up in his arms and hugged her to him for comfort then carried her back to the fire where he propped her up against the picnic basket.

His cool hands ran lightly over the rapidly swelling bulge above her foot. 'We have to bind that ankle. I don't think it's broken, but we'll get you X-rayed when we get back.

'You need an ice-pack, which we don't have, but I'll nip down to the river and get some cold water.' He left her and gathered up the empty wine bottle to fill with water.

When he returned from the river, he'd stripped off

his shirt and had it bundled, sodden in his hand, ready to wrap around her ankle. As he crouched beside her, intent on supporting the swelling, Bella diverted herself by the sight in front of her.

She'd never seen Scott without his shirt before. Maybe that had been good for her peace of mind— because she wasn't going to forget the sight in a hurry. His chest was deep and broad with only a fine sprinkle of dark hair across the tanned expanse, and she remembered the solid feel of the muscles in his arms when he'd carried her across to lay her down. His skin glistened in the firelight and it bronzed his tan even more.

There wasn't an ounce of spare fat to be seen as he knelt over her and in her dazed state she found her hand straying to trace the ridges of muscles in his abdomen. His skin was warm and firm under her fingers. She imagined him shirtless, rhythmically shaving wood in his workshop, the muscles bunching and relaxing with the sweep of the plane. Her head swam.

'Did I hurt you?' He stopped at her touch and she drew her hand back and shook her head.

'No. I just felt a bit faint. I needed to hang onto something.' She was glad the light from the fire wasn't shining on her face.

He smiled at her and Bella felt faint again. 'Your bedside manner is better than it was before,' she murmured.

He touched her cheek and returned to his bandaging and Bella had to admit the cold cloth felt heavenly against the heat in her ankle.

When he'd secured it as well as he could, Scott sat

back on his heels and looked at her. 'I'm guessing your ankle is throbbing like a drum full of knives. I think we need to change plans about staying until morning. How do you feel about me leaving you for a short while to try for some reception on my phone?'

Bella looked at the darkness at the edge of the circle of light they'd created. 'I'll be fine as long as a cow doesn't decide to walk all over me.'

'I could squeeze you into the back seat of the car with the windows down,' Scott offered, but she shook her head.

Despite the throbbing in her ankle, Bella smiled. 'Leave me a big stick and I'll be fine out here. It's too nice a night to be stuck in a car.'

He nodded and returned with two sticks, one magnificent wand-like branch and the other a shorter but sturdier one. 'One for playing with and one for business.' He put them beside her, as well as the wine bottle full of water and the jar of mango slices. He'd stripped the lambswool seat covers off the front seats of the car and made her a soft backrest and a fleecy mound to raise her leg on.

'I'll be as quick as I can. Call out if you need me. The sound should carry and I'll hotfoot it back to you.'

Bella looked up at him. He'd already come to her rescue once today. The image of Scott rushing to save her like a shirtless hero on a safari made her smile. 'I'd like to see that.'

Scott tapped her nose. 'Do not cry wolf,' he warned, but there was a smile behind his eyes. 'I'm looking for the rise we came over before the parking area. I shouldn't be long.'

Bella twisted her neck to watch him disappear with long strides and he was beyond the light within seconds. The moon was slowly rising and it wasn't as dark as it had been. She looked in the direction of the river and the sound of frogs and crickets seemed louder now that she was on her own. All this because she hadn't wanted Scott to kiss her. Actually, because she'd really wanted Scott to kiss her too much.

CHAPTER SEVEN

ON HIS return, Bella heard Scott's footsteps crunching on the gravel before she saw him. He loomed tall above her and his face was very dear and welcome as he stepped into the light.

'How did you go?' They said it at the same time and both smiled.

'I was fine.' Bella went first. 'Did you manage to speak to Rohan?'

He nodded as he crouched down beside her to look at her ankle. 'I had to go a bit further than I'd hoped to find reception, but he should be here in about an hour.'

He studied her face. 'How's the pain?'

'As long as I don't move my ankle—bearable. Thank you for taking such good care of me, Scott.' She looked away from his searching gaze.

His voice was gentle. 'If I hadn't frightened you, you wouldn't be in this predicament.'

She felt the blush in her cheeks and kept her head down. 'I overreacted. And was clumsy.' She plastered a smile on her face and looked up at him. 'Let's not talk about it any more. What did Rohan say?'

'Lots of things I'm not going to tell you.' He shook his head with a grin and looked across at the fire. 'I'd better build this fire up a bit so they can find us, then start collecting water so we can put it out when we go.'

Later, when Rohan's Range Rover nosed next to the bonnet of the Torana, they could see there were two occupants in the car. Scott scowled when he recognised the young man from Bella's house.

'I've brought Blake to be the mechanic because it's his car.' Rohan raised an eyebrow at Scott. 'I would have brought a shirt for you if I'd known you'd lost yours.' Rohan's eyes twinkled in the glare of the headlights and he ignored the frown on Scott's face.

He smiled at Bella as she waved from her seat on the tarpaulin. 'Hi, there, Bella. I've brought you some painkillers.' Rohan came and sat down beside her and handed the tablets over. 'What was that you were saying today about starting a rumour?'

She ignored her brother-in-law's question as she swallowed the pills. She wasn't looking forward to the moving bit to come. 'Thanks for these and for coming, Rohan.' She smiled weakly across at Rohan's companion. 'You, too, Blake.'

Blake leaned through the driver's window of the Torana and popped the bonnet before turning back to her. 'Vivie was beside herself, thought you'd had a crash,' he said, and grinned as he raised the red bonnet.

Bella shook her head. 'Poor Vivie. No. I just left the headlights on when we stopped and flattened the battery, then I fell down a rabbit hole.'

'One of those day's, eh?' Blake said with another grin. 'I'll leave the medical stuff to these guys and jump-start the car.' Blake walked around and leaned into the front seat of Rohan's car and pulled out the jumper leads. Efficiently he connected the two cars and started Rohan's car then climbed into the Torana and turned the engine over. It roared into life and Blake hopped out and disconnected the cars.

Scott knelt down beside Bella. 'Rohan and I will carry you together but I'm afraid this is going to be a little uncomfortable.'

'Typical doctor's understatement,' Bella mumbled under her breath.

'Put your arms around my neck and we'll be as gentle as we can.' Bella reached up and Scott's hands went beneath her and suddenly she was up against his chest again. His warmth surrounded her and she'd never felt so safe.

Strangely her ankle hardly hurt at all but maybe that was because Rohan supported it in the sheepskin and they eased her into the car with as little jerking as possible.

Bella caught Rohan's eyes as he watched Scott arrange her on the seat and she rushed into speech. 'That was pretty good. You guys should have been paramedics, though I probably could have walked.' It was all bravado because she wouldn't have been able to put her foot to the ground, but she hoped it would divert the knowing looks she was receiving from both Rohan and Blake.

Scott ignored the other two. 'I don't think so,' he said as he eased the other sheepskin behind her leg to wedge it from moving. 'Stop making a fuss.'

Bella's eyes widened at the unfairness of the comment. 'I did not make a fuss.'

'I know. I was teasing you. You've been very brave and I'll be pleased when they've X-rayed that ankle. I'll just go and make sure the fire's out.' He backed out of the car and Bella watched him go. He was so tall and efficient and he'd cared for her with kindness and compassion. She didn't notice that she sighed as he walked away. Rohan did.

Scott had actually been very calm about the whole cascade of events, she thought. If she had to be marooned with someone again, not that she was planning to be, she wouldn't mind if it was Scott. Of course, there wasn't much chance of that happening. The day had been a fiasco from start to finish. She'd be lucky if Scott wanted to talk to her after this night was over.

The click of seat belts from the front meant they were on their way and Bella gazed wistfully out of the window as the headlights made one final sweep of the area before pointing back to the road. Blake honked his horn as he overtook them in his car and his taillights gradually disappeared.

'Young fool,' Scott growled.

'Just young,' Rohan disagreed. Bella's ankle was too painful for her to enter the conversation. Thankfully Scott didn't pursue his vendetta against Blake and the conversation died a natural death.

When they arrived at the hospital, Scott seemed oblivious to the fact that he was shirtless and Bella was in his arms. Bella held herself stiffly although she felt like burying her face in his chest. To bury her face in his bare chest would actually be even nicer than burying it in his shirt, but she restrained herself.

The last thing she wanted was that feeling of being

the subject of the hastily terminated conversations she'd gone through last year. Hopefully any rumours would blow over before she came back to work.

After an hour's wait for X-ray results, the emergency doctor agreed with Scott and Rohan and pronounced her ankle bruised and strained but not broken.

When Scott carried her back to the car, most of the staff of Outpatients were there to wave them off. Bella could feel the heat of embarrassment all the way to the tops of her ears. Considering how seriously Scott had always taken public opinion, he seemed unfazed. It was another puzzling facet of his recent behaviour.

Rohan assured Scott that he could manage to get his sister-in-law to her room without Scott's help and dropped him at his house. Scott leaned through the window before they could drive away. 'I'll see you tomorrow morning before work, Bella. Keep that leg elevated.'

Rohan was remarkably restrained for the rest of the drive home and Bella sighed with relief. But she knew her sister would be given a full account of his suspicions. Bella didn't want to think about that upcoming conversation because she wasn't ready to examine her feelings for Scott Rainford on her own—let alone with anyone else.

Wednesday

The next morning, Bella's ankle was less swollen but just as painful. Vivie brought her breakfast in bed and even Aunt Sophie had made it up the stairs to see the invalid.

'The whole trip sounds like a disaster,' Sophie pronounced. 'It's hard to look attractive when you've sprained your ankle.'

'At least he took his shirt off to wrap around my ankle.' Bella couldn't resist the opportunity to shock Aunt Sophie, but she was dreaming.

A snort indicated that Sophie was unimpressed. 'If he took his trousers off, that would be something to write home about.'

'Aunt Sophie!' Typically her aunt had come out on top. 'Scott was a complete gentleman after I was injured.'

'And what about before?' Sophie shot back. Bella blushed and Sophie cackled. 'You've made my day. You wait till I see him.'

'Aunt Sophie, don't you dare say anything to Scott or I'll never talk to you again.'

'Eh?' Sophie said as she heaved herself to her feet and cupped a hand over her ear. 'What did you say? Can't hear you.'

Bella shook her head as she listened to her aunt chuckling and wheezing as she went down the stairs.

Ten minutes later there was another knock and Scott opened the door. 'Good morning, Bella. How's your leg this morning?'

He looked very handsome and Bella couldn't help the tide of colour that rose in her cheeks as she worried if Sophie had seen him come in.

'I'm fine. I think it's a little better,' she said.

Scott sat down on the edge of the bed. 'Sophie said it was still painful.' Bella's cheeks burned hotter.

'Can I check it or would you rather someone else looked after you?'

Bella frowned at his diffidence. 'Now, why would I want that?'

He shrugged and she pulled back the sheets to expose her legs. The bandages were still intact from the treatment in the emergency department and he nodded with approval at the pillow under her leg. He gently ran his fingers over the bandage. 'The swelling's gone down quicker than I thought it would.' He undid the bandage and his cool fingers ran gently over her swollen skin. 'It looks much better.'

Bella had been rehearsing what to say to Scott all night. She bit her lip. 'Scott?'

He looked up. 'Yes, Bella?' There was amusement behind his eyes as if he knew what she was going to say.

'I'm sorry for the inconvenience yesterday.'

His eyes twinkled and she realised again how different he looked when he wasn't being stern. 'Why? I invited myself and dared you to say no.'

Bella smiled. 'Yes, you did.' She decided on complete honesty. 'Well, truth be told, I wasn't really going until you invited yourself and then I couldn't get out of it.'

Scott laughed out loud and Bella thought how few times she'd seen him really laugh over the last month. He should do it more often—it made him look more like someone else she knew but she couldn't place the resemblance. It also made him even more gorgeous.

'I'd say we're equally to blame,' he said. 'Next

time we'll take my car. The Volvo beeps when I leave the lights on.'

Bella bit her lip at the thought of more day trips with Scott. She didn't know how she felt about that idea. She left it at a noncommittal, 'We'll see.' Luckily Scott didn't pursue the conversation.

'Keep that foot elevated today. How's the pain, really?' he asked.

'A little easier and those pills Rohan gave me help, but they make me vague.'

'Keep taking them today. If you rest properly you might be able to get up tomorrow.' He glanced at his watch and stood up. 'By the way, I rang the local bus service and they'll donate a driver for your youth bus this week.'

She felt like bursting into tears that he'd thought to do that for her, which was ridiculous. It was probably those stupid pills that made her emotions so fragile. Bella bit her lip and looked up at him. 'Thank you.'

'Rest,' he said, and left. Bella stared at the spot where he'd disappeared and then glanced at the clock to see how many hours until he came back. When she realised what she'd done she closed her eyes and called herself all kinds of fool.

There was another knock on the door and she opened her eyes. She wouldn't be lonely, she thought, and straightened her blankets and called for whoever it was to come in. Blake poked his head around the door but didn't enter the room.

'Hi, Bella.' He smiled and Bella couldn't help the feeling of *déjà vu* that trickled down her spine. He'd taken the eyebrow stud out, shaved and cut his hair, and it made him look older and infinitely more wholesome. 'Who is this gorgeous young man at my door?' she teased.

'It was Vivie's idea,' Blake said, and he ran his hand through the short brown spikes on his head. 'What do you think?'

'You'll get a swollen head if I tell you what I think.'

Blake blushed. 'I just wanted to know if you needed anything in town today.' He shrugged. 'Books, magazines, fruit?'

Bella indicated the chair beside the bed. 'Thanks for the offer, Blake. How about a conversation instead?' Anything to get her mind away from her last visitor. 'Can you spare me ten minutes?'

Blake shrugged again and walked across the room. He spun the chair backwards to straddle it. 'Sure.'

Bella watched him sit and his boyish enthusiasm made her feel old. 'I'm always rushing about and I haven't had a chance to ask you how you're settling in. So, tell me, how do you find living in a house full of women?'

Blake laughed. 'Actually, it's fun. I always wanted a sister, and it's like having six of them.'

'I've two sisters,' Bella said. 'Abbey you know and a younger one, Kirsten. She's due back from Saudi Arabia soon. Do you have any brothers?'

'Nope. And both my parents were only children as well. They were in their fifties when I arrived but they always had time to sit and talk to me. I miss that the most.' He kept his head up but there was a suspicion of moisture in his eyes.

'You sound very proud of them,' Bella said gently.

'I was…am. They were wonderful people. Dad died last year and my mum died a few months later. I miss them both.' He looked away and then back at Bella. 'They didn't own their own home and by the time I paid all the bills there wasn't much left to stay in Sydney for. I decided to come up here.'

Bella nodded. 'My parents died when I was a couple of years younger than you. Losing them was horrible. But I wasn't alone like you were. I've always had Abbey and she looked after Kirsten and me. Later on Aunt Sophie moved in with us as well. I can't imagine not having any family.'

He shrugged and then stood up. 'I don't need anyone.' He glanced across at Bella. His statement hung in the air for a moment, then he said, 'Can I ask you a question?'

Bella smiled. 'If I don't like it I won't answer.'

'Fair enough.' Blake stared down at the carpet. 'Are you and Dr Rainford going out together?'

Bella shook her head and then realised he couldn't see her answer. 'No. We're not. Dr Rainford thinks he's too old for me.'

She glanced across at Blake's face and saw his brows draw together and the dark frown made his face so incredibly like Scott's that she drew in a sharp breath. It had to be coincidence but since Blake had lost his beard and long hair the similarities between both men screamed out at Bella. No wonder she'd felt Blake was familiar—he looked a lot like Scott had when she'd first met him.

Blake was oblivious to Bella's shock. 'What about you? Do you think he's too old for you?' he said.

Despite her racing brain, Bella had to smile. 'I've never thought he was too old.'

'So you've fancied him for a while?' Blake certainly wanted the ins and outs. Bella laughed. 'I think this is where I say I'm not answering.'

Blake glanced across and grinned. 'OK.'

'I've got a question.' Bella wondered if she was mad but the conviction was growing. Now every time Blake's face changed expression he looked like Scott.

'Do you have a middle name, Blake?' It was a long shot and she didn't really have the right to pry.

'Why do you want to know?' He was more guarded and Bella trod carefully.

'Just curious. You don't have to tell me if you don't want to.'

'Michael,' he said, and Bella nodded.

Her voice softened. 'And what did you find out in Sydney that made you want to come up here?'

Unconsciously, Blake glanced towards the door. 'What are you getting at?'

'I wondered if you were searching for something— or someone.' She saw his knuckles tighten on the back of the chair and she didn't know how it could be but she knew that what she suspected was true.

'I don't want to answer that.' Blake's mouth had hardened.

'No problem.' Bella watched the suspicion grow in his eyes and she backed off. 'I've been meaning to say how much I enjoyed driving your car.'

Blake followed her lead in the change of subject but the suspicion was still there. He nodded. 'I like it. Sorry it died on you.'

'I often wonder if things happen for a reason,'

Bella mused, and Blake let go of the chair and jingled his keys. He couldn't hide his eagerness to escape.

'If you don't want anything from town then I'll be going,' he said.

'No. I don't need anything. Thanks for asking,' said Bella, and he left. Vivie met him at the door but he didn't stop. Blake edged past her to disappear down the stairs a little faster than normal.

Vivie looked after him wistfully and then came into Bella's room with another cup of tea. Bella would be floating by this afternoon if she didn't stop drinking the stuff. 'Thanks, Vivie.'

Bella had to consciously avoid asking questions about Blake but the temptation was there. Fifteen minutes later Vivie left and Bella took two pills for the pain in her ankle but she knew she wouldn't sleep for a while as she mulled over her suspicions. Should she tell Scott?

When Abbey and baby Lachlan came to visit, the sisters talked about babies and motherhood for a while. It was Abbey who broached the subject they'd both been avoiding.

'Do you need to talk about Scott?' she asked, and Bella shook her head.

She should have known Abbey would instinctively offer to listen but not pressure her to answer.

'No, I'd like to get it straight in my mind.'

Abbey nodded though she still looked concerned. 'I still believe he did the right thing twelve years ago but I can see you are both different people now. I'm here to listen if you need me.'

Bella nodded and Abbey didn't stay much longer.

*　*　*

When Scott called in again that evening after work Bella had had time to think. There hadn't been much else to do stuck in bed. Unless Blake decided to confirm her suspicions, nothing would be gained by Bella's interference. The most she could do was try to help Scott see the young man in a more positive light.

'Vivie tells me Blake has been to see Melissa and her baby every day. That's pretty good for a young guy who's not the father of the child.'

Scott wasn't receptive when she mentioned Blake's sterling qualities. 'I came to see how your ankle was, not discuss him.' He cocked an eyebrow. 'I thought your house guests were none of my business anyway.'

Bella could have stamped her foot in frustration except it would have hurt. Instead, she gave up. 'My leg is fine. How was the ward?'

Scott frowned at her. 'The ward will be fine. Will you stop worrying about everyone else and just relax? The world won't stop turning because you're not there to sacrifice yourself.'

Bella glared at him. 'I don't sacrifice myself. I chose my life. And you're the last person who should talk about sacrificing.'

Scott shook his head. 'Now you sound like Rohan. And I didn't come here to bicker with you.'

Bella paused then asked, 'Why did you come, then?'

'To see that you were improving. I was also going to offer a run in my car on Saturday if you wanted to get out after being inside for a few days. But if you're as cantankerous as you are now, I won't worry.' The new, teasing Scott smiled at her and she could feel the traitorous melting feeling she seemed to have been afflicted with over the last few days every time Scott entered her vicinity.

Bella stopped and stared at him. Did she want to spend more time alone with Scott?

Unfortunately, yes.

She couldn't help the flutter of excitement in her stomach that accelerated as she considered his invitation. Yes. She'd like that. But she wasn't going to do anything she might regret later. 'I think I'd enjoy that. Thank you for thinking of me.'

He stood up. 'I have to go to Port Macquarie for a conference tomorrow and Friday, so I'll catch you Saturday, then? Say about ten?'

Bella nodded and smiled to hide the realisation that she was actually going to miss not seeing him tomorrow. Maybe she'd be better to cancel now because this was more serious than she'd anticipated. All these emotions from a few hours in his company had become dangerous territory.

It was almost as if he had read her thoughts, he said, 'It's just a trip to get you out.'

Later that night, when all the lights in the house were out, Bella lay and stared at the ceiling.

She thought about her relationship with Scott when she'd been eighteen, from the perspective of an almost thirty-year-old woman, and saw it for what it was—young adoring love on her part. She wasn't sure, but probably it had been infatuation on Scott's part. She just couldn't figure out why he'd encouraged her in the first place if he'd been unwilling to trust his instinct.

Realistically, she was starting to fall under his spell

again, and she didn't know if she could trust him not to hurt her again.

Was she going to choose to let Scott into her life with all the risks that entailed if he cooled off again like he had twelve years ago?

Bella closed her eyes determinedly and willed herself to go to sleep. She was the one responsible for her own happiness—not him. She'd just have to go with her instincts.

Saturday

Come Saturday morning, Bella stared out the window at the lack of rainclouds. Not one to be seen in a blue, blue sky. She'd have to go. The simmering excited side of her smiled but the sensible, wary side shook in its sensible boots.

When Scott arrived, the sensible Bella was waiting, unsmiling, in light trousers and a T-shirt at the kitchen table. Her ankle was almost better, but she'd strapped it and wasn't planning to overstretch it today because she needed to be right by Monday for work. She had to admit, though, Scott had been close to the mark about her going stir-crazy from being house bound.

'How was the conference?' Bella asked, and gathered her handbag and sunglasses.

He smiled. 'Fine. Have you been so bored you missed me?'

'Just bored,' Bella said as she walked carefully through the door Scott held open for her.

She stepped out into the sunlight with a feeling of relief to escape from the house but couldn't help a little trepidation at the thought of what she was going to say today.

Bella planned to be careful, go for the ride and come home heart whole and with some answers. While Scott concentrated on the traffic she stared at him thoughtfully.

He seemed relaxed today and the curve of his lips made Bella's mouth twitch. What was it about him that reached out and pressed all the right buttons? In her eyes he really hadn't changed much since she'd first known him except for his assurance. Now he carried himself as if he was accustomed to the responsibilities that rested on his shoulders. Responsibilities that he took seriously, to the extent that he was the person always available when needed, the local doctor who attended the most house calls and did the most after-hours calls. He'd always said that the town was his family and Bella suddenly realised how much they'd all relied on him over the years.

Externally, she couldn't see the drain it must have been on him. His chin had always been ruggedly square and seriously dark brows hovered ready to exclaim or frown above his jungle-green eyes. Even his hair remained black-coffee brown with no sprinkling of the grey that should have been there and no clue to the passing of years. He had such broad shoulders. Her gaze lingered.

The sudden memory of after she'd turned her ankle, the breadth of his chest as he'd easily carried her, the strength in his arms and the gentleness in his hands, twisted in her stomach and made her look away from him. She stared out of the window to lecture herself on finding that aloofness she'd decided to hide behind today.

'Do I pass muster?' There was a teasing note in his voice.

Bella looked back at him and met his next glance and smiled. She needed to stop feeling like a silly teenager around this man. 'You've always been attractive to me, Scott.'

Startled, he flicked a glance back at her and she was glad she'd spoken out. Every time she'd said what she thought, things seemed to improve between them. Though she was going to test that theory to its limit today. 'I was just trying to work out why.'

'Tell me about it,' he joked, and she frowned. Scott's insecurities had never been a factor in her rationalisation of the heartbreak she'd suffered at his hands.

She took a quiet breath to steady her voice. 'Maybe today would be a good time to clear out the cobwebs and get rid of some of the things I've never understood.'

'About what?' He asked the question but Bella had the feeling he knew what she meant.

'About what happened between us twelve years ago.' Bella watched his face in profile and she couldn't tell how her suggestion had been received.

'Perhaps,' he said, and the silence lengthened between them as she let him ponder her statement. Bella was content to wait.

The scenery flashed past. A farmer on a motorbike rounded up his cattle and she smiled at a blue cattle dog nipping around the edges of another herd. Then they turned off the road towards South West Rocks and Scott broke the silence between them.

'I thought we might go up to the lighthouse first, check out the view and maybe have a coffee. Which I remembered to bring,' Scott said.

'Lucky, after last time.' Bella nodded and they both smiled at the memory of her mock complaint at their last picnic.

The car wound slowly through the dim rain-forest drive up to Smokey Cape Lighthouse and Bella couldn't resist opening her window to feel the cool moist air of the heavy vegetation. The sound of cicadas and birds drifted into the car. She thought she caught a glimpse of a lyre bird but it was gone before she could point it out to Scott.

They popped out into the sunlight beneath the lighthouse and the sea stretched away in three directions past the headlands.

Scott stopped the car for a minute while Bella soaked in the view with a smile on her face. 'I'm so glad I came. I'd forgotten how lush and beautiful it is along that road and then this.' She spread her hands and her gaze travelled along the horizon and back again.

'Me, too,' Scott said, but he was looking at Bella. 'It's easy to forget what you have in your own back yard.'

Scott manoeuvred his car into the highest spot in the car park and then came around to open her door.

'I thought we could sit at one of the tables and watch for whales.'

'Thank you,' Bella murmured as he shut the car door behind her. 'I've never seen a whale.'

He nodded. 'I don't really think they go past here at all.' She laughed because she knew that they did. He lifted the familiar basket onto the picnic table, and this time he produced a Thermos of steaming coffee. 'Percolated!'

She shook her head. 'You're having me on.'

Scott grinned. 'Ground this morning. Of course, it's never as good as the freshly made stuff but we'll see.'

Bella sniffed the contents of her mug and the aroma was strong and rich. The azure sea stretched away to meet the lighter colour of the sky and a white-capped sea eagle circled overhead.

She sighed with pleasure. 'I could get used to this.'

Scott gazed out to sea as well. 'When I think of all the weekends I haven't done something like this, it makes me feel I should count the ones that are left.'

Bella frowned. 'That's a little morbid, isn't it? I'd prefer to think of it as thank goodness I remembered to come here, and I'm definitely going to try and come more often. Even knowing this is all here enriches my soul.'

'Pollyanna strikes again.'

She shook her head. 'It's more than positive thinking. It's accepting that life is full of experiences, good and bad. We aren't victims of fate because we can choose how we deal with those experiences.'

'Some people don't deal as well with life experiences as others.' Scott looked away and then back at Bella again. 'Take love, for instance. What have you learnt from love?'

Bella raised her chin. 'From love?' Her voice lowered and he had to strain to hear her. 'All bad things,' she said. 'It's taken me a long time to rebuild my self-esteem and for the moment I choose to stand alone.'

Scott winced at the part he'd played in her disillusionment. 'So you're never going to get involved with a man again?'

She shook her head vehemently. 'I didn't say that. I'm just not going to lose myself in the process.' She tilted her chin. 'And if I find someone, he'll get a better bargain. Not some wimpy clinging vine.'

'I used to like vines,' he mused. 'A woman's arms hanging on. There's a halfway mark, you know. Some vines are so strong people can grow with them.'

She smiled. 'Nice analogy. I was getting a bit serious there. Sorry.'

He shook his head and captured her chin in his hand. 'You were telling me how you feel. And I'm privileged that you feel you can talk to me.' He let her go.

Their eyes met and there was silence for a moment as everything from the past seemed to shimmer between them. 'I've always felt I could talk to you,' she said.

He refilled her cup. 'In the car you said you wanted to clear out cobwebs and old misunderstandings. What sort of cobwebs?'

Bella looked at him thoughtfully. 'Big cobwebs. Huge cobwebs. Cobwebs like why you let me think I meant something to you twelve years ago then abandoned me. Then told Abbey to keep me away from you.'

'Oh,' he said. 'Those cobwebs.'

CHAPTER EIGHT

'It's a long story but I guess we have time,' Scott said, and cast his mind back to a time that had made a great impact on his life.

Twelve years ago, Bella and her two sisters had stood at their mother's grave like red-haired nuns dressed in black. Abbey, the oldest, had been slightly bowed but upright under the weight of responsibility. Kirsten, the youngest, had looked confused and angry and her eyes had searched for answers. But Bella, frighteningly beautiful like her mother, had been completely lost.

Scott looked at her now. That young girl was long gone.

He removed the coffee-cup from her hand and took her fingers in his. He held them lightly as if he needed to feel her hand in his to tell this story.

'I remember the first day I saw you. It was your mother's funeral. You stood totally crushed, like a bruised and bewildered flame-headed butterfly, impaled on a tragedy too great for you to grasp. When I looked into your eyes that day, something shifted— irrevocably—and it didn't matter how hard I tried to tell myself it wasn't so.'

Bella felt the tears film her eyes as she listened. It was as if they were both standing in that moment of time. She could almost feel the nip in the air and the moisture from the rain that had fallen just before the service. And she could remember that look. The compassion in his eyes had soothed her as nothing during those terrible days had been able to do.

He went on. 'I'd lost my mother years before and I understood how devastating it was for you. I went home that night and I couldn't sleep. I told myself that I'd just help you.' His mouth curved cynically.

'I was so much older than you.' He looked at her. 'I'm still so much older than you,' he said dryly, and they both laughed at the ridiculousness of the statement.

It lightened the mood for a moment and they smiled at each other before he squeezed her hand and continued. 'I'd made mistakes, big mistakes, and you were so young and pure and so deserving of the best that life could offer you. I've never thought of myself as the best.' He stared straight ahead.

'I was brought up by a rich uncle and aunt who did what was necessary and sent me to the best schools, and I'm grateful for that. But I'd never felt as if I belonged anywhere until I moved here and the town welcomed me with open arms.

'Everyone trusted me and here I was contemplating the seduction of a vulnerable teenager.' He put her hand back in her lap and sat up as if the next part was harder to talk about.

'I was weak in the beginning because you needed so much comfort and I told myself I could step back when you were less destroyed by your loss. But the more I saw you the more you offered me, and if I hadn't stepped back I would have lost my head and we would have been lovers. I would have demanded you marry me, and I have first-hand experience of how such age-disparate marriages can fail. I couldn't risk the pain I'd experienced falling to you if our marriage failed. I cared for you too much to see you wish you'd never married me.' The starkness in his voice told her that he meant every word he said, and Bella spared a dark thought for the woman who had made him doubt himself so badly.

'Why didn't you talk to me about it?' Bella's voice thickened with tears and memories.

'I knew if I explained that to you then, you'd have said we should be together. You deserved more.'

She shook her head in denial. 'What did you tell Abbey and why?'

'I told her we were too close and that I was too old for you. Telling Abbey was the only way to make the break permanent.' He snorted with self-derision. 'I knew she would agree. That time you came back to my house we were playing with fire and that's why I had to send you away.'

Scott shifted on the seat. 'Abbey was the only one I knew who was strong enough to help.'

A single tear slid down Bella's cheek unheeded by her. 'What if I'd said you were all I ever wanted?'

He stroked the drop from her cheek until it disappeared. 'I wouldn't have believed you. Still wouldn't believe you.'

She nodded and stared out to sea again. Then it was hopeless all over again. All she said was, 'That explains a lot.' And left it at that.

'You said there were a few things you wanted clar-
ified today?'

She couldn't take any more of his reasons for not
loving her. 'Maybe later.' She dropped her cup in the
picnic basket and stood up, suddenly needing to leave
this place and the things that had been said. In fact,
a slow anger was building and she needed to distract
herself. 'Where else are we going today, driver?'

Scott shook his head. She amazed him and frustrated him and he couldn't read the mixed signals he
was getting. This day was becoming more painful
than he had bargained for as he could sense the beginnings of a horrible feeling that maybe he had done
the wrong thing all those years ago to turn Bella
away. That concept had implications for the negative
experiences Bella had been through, which he didn't
want to think about, and he concentrated on manual
tasks to divert his thoughts.

After he'd repacked the car, they drove down towards the town of South West Rocks along the back
road at Arakoon, then past the new country club and
into town.

'Do you want to eat at a restaurant or take-away
on the headland?' Scott left it up to Bella because
suddenly he didn't know what he had planned. This
day was spinning out of control faster than he could
have imagined.

Bella glanced up the side road that ran up to the
lookout. 'I used to have fish and chips on the headland with my family when Mum and Dad were alive.
Let's do that.'

Scott nodded and parked in the parking area above the beach.

Horseshoe Bay was small and had a bluff of rock pools at one end and tumbled boulders at the other. Between was a curve of white sand in the shape of a horseshoe. Tall pine trees overlooked the grassed areas that ran almost down to the beach, popular with young families and older couples.

Today it boasted a dozen families and the lifeguard in charge was busy keeping the swimmers within the flags.

Bella pointed to a spot in the middle of the bay. 'I was caught in a rip there once. But it was a weekday and there wasn't a lifeguard.'

Scott looked out where she indicated and there was nothing to make it look dangerous.

'I can remember it as plainly as if it were yesterday. I was only about nine. Dad was swimming with Abbey. Kirsten was stung by a bluebottle in the shallows at the same time as I must have paddled across the rip.' She pointed to a darker line in the water. 'There's a rip.' She looked back at him. 'Mum was trying to calm Kirsten and Dad went to help her. The rip pulled me out into the deeper water before I knew it and suddenly I couldn't make any headway towards the beach and everybody on the beach seemed further away. I was terrified and tired from trying to swim against the undercurrent.'

She shivered at the memory. 'All of a sudden Abbey appeared beside me and told me to stop fighting the pull and we'd slip out the side of the rip in a little while.'

She looked towards the tumbled boulders. 'We climbed out of the water over there and I was crying and Abbey was telling me how clever I was to hang on for so long. But I knew if it hadn't been for her I would have drowned.'

She shook her head at the memories and smiled. 'Dad made us join junior lifesavers that summer to learn about safety in the sea, but I never enjoyed it much.' She laughed. 'Abbey used to win the races all the time. It's funny, the things that affect your life.'

Scott steered her towards a park bench and they sat down overlooking the bay. 'I wish I could have been there for you.'

'Abbey was there.' Bella shrugged. 'She's always been there. I guess that was why it was so devastating when I was attacked last year. I was already hurting from discovering that the man I loved had lied to me for three years. I was on the way to Abbey and her safe haven and then something even worse happened. I thought nothing more horrible could happen than that, and I blamed Abbey for not saving me. Until Abbey was nearly shot by that madman. Ironically, in the process of saving Abbey and Rohan, I saved myself.

'From not being able to look myself in the mirror, suddenly I could hold my head high. I realised that I do have power and that was when I decided that I would choose how to let things affect me.'

He stared at her. 'You've come a long way. You deserve to be proud of the woman you are now.'

'I am proud. And I'm careful. So I won't be rush-

ing into anything.' Her words hung in the air between them.

She brushed away an ant that had climbed along
the seat. 'Enough about me.' She turned to face him
and the sun was shining in her hair and the fierceness
in her eyes had been replaced by compassion.

'Tell me about your marriage, Scott.'

He didn't want to but maybe it was time for him
to leave the past behind as well. He rubbed his chin.
'My marriage was a poor choice in a long line of poor
choices. I was looking for a family, and a sense of
belonging that I never had with my aunt and uncle.
Maybe even a mother like the one I lost.'

He laughed bitterly and Bella put her hand on his
arm. 'I don't know why Madeline married me but,
whatever the reason, the reason went away and she
couldn't get out of the marriage fast enough.'

Bella tilted her head. 'Maybe the pregnancy scared
her?'

Scott grimaced. 'It seems likely in hindsight. We
really had nothing in common but I would have stood
by her. She didn't have a termination so it wasn't that
she didn't want our son either.'

'Maybe she was protecting you?'

Scott couldn't see the logic in that. 'From what?'

Bella frowned at his lack of insight. 'From throwing away your life on her and a new baby. Did you
ever say anything about not wanting children?'

He stared into the distant past. 'Who knows? I
could have. I was young and selfish and determined
to finish uni. We were fighting. Maybe I said something about being glad we didn't have children to hear

the shouting. I don't remember, but it's not outside the realms of possibility. Perhaps she decided she wanted the child and not the father. I'll never know. I know that she ended up hating me so much she kept the birth of my son from me. I just wish she'd given me the chance to find out if I could be a decent father.'

Bella heard the bitterness in his voice. 'So Michael would be around the same age you were when you married his mother.'

He looked at her. 'I guess you're right.' He turned to watch a toddler splashing at the water's edge. 'I see a child like that little fellow and think how I missed out on seeing Michael that age.' He shifted his gaze to a young boy throwing a ball. 'And that age.' And then to a young man and his girlfriend at the next bench. 'To now.'

Bella nodded. 'So how do you imagine him now?'

Scott stared at the people swimming between the flags. 'I admit that in the last fortnight, if I see a young man walk down the street I think that I could walk right by him and not recognise him as my son. It's not a nice feeling.'

'Do you think he'd recognise you?'

He smiled. 'Do you mean an older face in the mirror?' He thought about it. 'It's a nice idea.' He laughed. 'And pretty scary for him.'

'You really are age-obsessed, aren't you?' She said the words lightly but he took them to heart.

'I don't even want to go there.' This was too close to naming the reason for all the mistakes he'd made. He wasn't sure of the final tally and what that admission could cost. He stood up. 'Let's find fish and chips.' Scott brushed off the negatives. The pain of catharsis, he thought cynically.

Then she cast her spell over him again and he couldn't help thinking of all the years they'd missed out on.

They sat on a blanket on the grassy headland over-looking the main beach and ate out of the white paper wrapping. The long crescent of sand stretched away in the distance to Trial Bay where the ruins of the old penal settlement were stark above the convict-built break wall. They munched hot golden chips and crunchy pieces of freshly fried fish covered in salt and lemon juice, and when he was finished Scott watched Bella lick the salt from her fingers. The savage twist in his stomach ensured that he turned away.

He looked back when she'd finished. 'You are tor-turing me, you know that?' he said.

Bella cocked an eyebrow at him and there was nothing childlike in the glance she sent him. 'Good. You deserve it. When I think of the devastation I suffered at your hands, I'm glad.'

He laughed out loud at her sudden defiance and reached across to steal the longest of her chips.

'Hey, I was saving that one.' She glared at him and tried to snatch it back but his arms were longer than hers and she brushed against him delightfully.

'Good,' he said, and dangled it closer so she'd reach again for the chip. When she was off balance he slipped his arm around her and pulled her onto his lap so that she was looking into his face. He dropped a kiss on her salty lips, and her eyes widened in surprise. He flicked the clasp out of her hair and then rolled her back onto her side of the rug so that he was leaning over her with her hair spread out behind her.

She looked so beautiful and vibrant, but despite his position of power he had the feeling she was nowhere near intimidated by him. 'What are you going to do about that?' he dared her.

'I could be very nasty from this position,' she warned with a glint in her eye, and Scott laughed and rolled off her.

'Ah, the self-defence classes.' He sat up again and offered his hand. 'Women's lib is such a pain.'

She let him help her up and finger-combed her hair back into its clasp.

'But useful.' She stared at him thoughtfully. 'Where do you think this new rapport we seem to have found is going?'

He shrugged and wouldn't meet her eyes and Bella's self-protective instincts kicked in when he said, 'I'm not sure. Does it have to go somewhere or can we just start again as friends?'

'What sort of friends, Scott?' There was a snap in her voice. 'It's a great idea but what about the fact that I seem to end up in your arms when I least expect it? That's not friendly, that's chemistry.'

He met her eyes and the warmth in his look felt like a breeze from the equator across her skin. She had no control over the way he could sear her with a glance. 'See!' she said.

He smiled and captured her hand between his.

'We've always had that and I don't know why. But at least I'm looking for an answer.'

Bella bit her lip. 'Well, I'm not looking for heartache again, Scott.'

Scott looked at her. 'I hear you when you say you don't want to fall into heartache. But if you fall I will catch you. I won't ever drop you again.'

She frowned. 'Am I the only one who thinks this change in our relationship is too sudden? I'm not sure I can trust you.' Bella shook her head and screwed up the paper roll her chips had come in.

He spread his hands. 'So how do you think we should do this?'

She met his eyes and the wariness was still there on her side. 'We'll see how we go.' She took one more look at the horizon and stood up. 'Thank you for the day. I'd like to go home now, please.'

Sunday

Sunday was for thinking and weighing up and having space to consider what it would mean to trust Scott not to hurt her again. And to realise even those few times in the last week they'd spent together had been enough to fan the attraction she'd always felt towards him. She needed to accept that he was her weakness.

It wasn't fair and it wasn't sensible but she needed to admit that she would always love Scott Rainford—and that she was falling 'in love' again.

Unfortunately she still had the same problem she'd had twelve years ago—he wasn't ready to commit to anything or tell the world he was in love with a younger woman, and she'd grown up enough to realise she deserved more. It didn't look promising.

She could stay firm and avoid Scott out of work hours but realistically when he turned the heat on she was like ice cream in the sun. A sticky puddle of indecision.

When the phone rang that afternoon, Bella took it in the hallway, fully expecting it to be for one of the girls.

'Hello?' She absently picked up a pen to take a message.

'Bella?' Scott's voice jerked her out of her daydream and into confusion.

She was hopeless. The least she could do was not let him know that. 'Yes, who is this?'

'It's Scott!'

She could hear the frown in his voice when he answered and she suppressed her smile.

'Yes, Scott. What can I do with you?' She stopped and replayed what she'd said in her head and winced. 'I mean, *for* you.'

'We'd better not go with the first one,' he teased, his good humour restored, and she felt like stamping her foot. She was nearly thirty years old. She should be calm and collected on the end of the phone.

He went on, 'I wondered if you'd like to come around. I've a chilled Verdello, we could eat Chinese take-away and share the sunset before we dive into another hectic week on the ward.'

'I don't drink and drive.' It was true and convenient.

He wasn't fazed. 'Then I'll pick you up and send you home in a taxi.'

She was going to say no but he must have sensed that. 'It's a pretty radical thing to do, to catch a taxi home on a Sunday night.'

Bella weakened. All the memories of that wonderful afternoon by the river came back and teased her. But she needed more time to think things through before she did her moth impersonation and circled his light bulb again.

'I don't think so, Scott.' But she couldn't help the indecision in her voice.

'One drink and dinner then I'll send you home.'

She could go or she could stay home and wish she had gone. Hard decision. 'I hope the taxi charges you double for weekend rates.'

'Fine,' he said. 'I'll be there in half an hour to pick you up.' The phone went dead.

Bella stared at the handset as if it were responsible for the panic she was in now. Today was supposed to be for reflection.

By the time she'd changed, told Vivie she wouldn't be home for tea, changed again because she didn't want to look like she'd changed, and spent ten minutes talking to herself in the mirror and promising not to get into any close clinches with Scott, he was there. She couldn't believe she was dumb enough to do this when he'd blatantly told her he just wanted to be friends.

'Have you ordered dinner yet?' She clicked the car seat belt into the locking mechanism and turned to face him.

He looked at her sideways. 'It's home delivery. They'll bring it when I ring. Are you in a hurry?'

'I don't want it to be a late night.' Bella stared straight ahead.

He glanced at his watch. 'It's five-thirty. I could probably have you in bed by seven.'

Bella jerked her head to look at him in shock and he took his hands off the steering-wheel briefly to ask the question, 'What?' Then he realised what he'd said and bit his lip, but his eyes were laughing.

'I meant to bed in your house—not mine.'

Bella felt like an idiot but she took a deep breath and tried to calm down. She'd worked herself into such a state and she'd been so focussed yesterday. That's what was really getting to her. She'd lost the plot and yesterday she'd had it all under control.

Scott sensed her turmoil. 'Relax. We'll have a pleasant evening and I'll send you home in a taxi.' He should never have asked her to come, Scott thought. She wasn't ready and he was pressuring her. He was a fool and there was a real risk that they'd do something she or he could regret. He didn't want that. 'Would you like me to take you home now?'

Yes, she thought. 'No, I'm fine,' she said.

It was a little easier when they arrived at his house. They walked around the garden to see which shrubs were flowering at the moment, and by the time they were back on the verandah Bella was feeling more in control. A large glass of Verdello helped.

The conversation flowed and they slipped into the old rapport that had been such a big part of their relationship all those years ago. Bella only had to half explain things and Scott understood the nuances and why.

But there was more humour between them now and the longer they talked the more relaxed Bella became.

The sun slowly sank over the river and they leaned on the verandah rail to enjoy the cascade of changing colours against the mountains in the distance. When the sun had set she sighed.

'I think we should eat.' Bella stared into her empty glass and Scott nodded.

'I've really enjoyed this, Bella,' he said. 'Come through into the lounge while I phone the restaurant. You can choose some music while we wait.'

Bella found some ballads that suited her mood and she flitted around the furniture admiring Scott's carpentry, still awed by the fact that he had furnished his house with his own creations. She wandered across to the mantelpiece where there was one single photo of Scott as a young man, flanked by an older couple. The resemblance to Blake was striking.

He came back into the room and tucked his wallet back into his trousers. 'What shall we do while we wait?'

'Is this your aunt and uncle?'

He crossed the room to her and stared at the photo. 'Yes. I was about seventeen. I've changed a bit since then.'

Bella stared at the photo. 'Not that much. Your hair was lighter and, of course, your build was more slight. Your son probably looks like that now.'

She saw him frown as he stared at the photo with more attention. She wondered if he could see the resemblance between the photo and Blake as he was now. Would Scott comment on the similarities between Blake and himself, and should she tell him her own thoughts? Bella didn't know what to do. 'What are you thinking?' she asked instead.

He looked at her and then back at the photo. 'It's nothing. A crazy thought.' Her heart rate accelerated and then settled when he shook his head to shrug it off. Then he smiled at her and subtly the mood in the room changed.

'Where were we?' he said.

Bella turned her back to him before he saw the awareness in her eyes. 'Monopoly?' She offered.

'Maybe I should just take you home now and they can deliver your part of the Chinese food to your house.'

'That's always an option.' Bella talked to the safety of the mantelpiece in front of her.

His voice came from behind her shoulder and although he wasn't touching her she could feel the heat from his body next to hers and the vibration of energy between them.

'You should be wary but we won't do anything you don't want to do, Bella,' he said, but they both knew that wasn't the problem.

'It's not *your* control I'm worried about, Scott,' she said dryly, and turned to face him. Bad idea.

He was very close. They stared at each other and she shook her head. 'Why do I feel as if I'm going to regret this if I do and regret it if I don't?'

'What are you talking about?' he said, and moved back a pace.

'I think you should just kiss me and let the rest work itself out.' Bella watched his eyes widen and his hands went back behind his body in denial.

'I don't think that's a good idea.'

Her eyes burned into his. 'Please?'

He shut his eyes for a moment and then leaned forward and stroked her cheek. 'Ah, Bella. I need to take you home because we're not ready for this. You don't know all the disadvantages there are to being with me.'

Bella had made her choice. She captured his finger and kissed it, and he froze. Then, unable to help himself, he slid his hand around her neck and pulled her close against him.

'One kiss,' he said, and lowered his mouth to hers. And the next time she breathed he was there. But it was never going to be one kiss if Bella had her way.

Nibbles of desire flickered along her limbs with every taste of his mouth. Every whisper of breath between them lifted the stakes higher.

She had to choose now or lay the blame at his door like the weakling she'd always been. She chose to raise the stakes.

If she didn't hold him now, properly, then any chance she had of convincing him that they were right together would be gone for ever, Bella feared. There was liberation in that commitment and she felt as if a weight had gone from her shoulders. She would live with the consequences.

She returned his kiss fiercely and he froze for a second as his arms went around her and she sighed against him. This was what she wanted and needed and, judging by the firmness of Scott's hold, he was in no hurry to let her go.

The taste of him entwined with the pressure of his mouth and created an enthralling environment any promptings of Bella's sanity couldn't compete against.

This *was* what she wanted, and what she'd been afraid of. Her hands crept up to his neck and threaded in his hair. His long fingers splayed across her hips and she was crushed against him. It was like a home-coming and she pressed herself closer, revelling in the danger.

Scott's mouth seduced and enticed her like a duel-list and Bella cherished the possessive way he held her against him. Possessive yet with such sweetness that she felt the tears sting her eyes.

The music from the stereo flickered through her consciousness to match the kindling flames that flashed and roared inside her in time to the now rhyth-mic plundering of her mouth by his. Scott claimed her in a way that erased every kiss any other man had given her. The magic he created opened up a range of sensations that had her dazzled.

She moaned and whispered his name. Her body swayed as she leaned into him. To be in Scott's arms was everything she'd dreamed it would be.

Scott was in deep trouble. Here was the woman he'd always loved, adored from afar, yielding in his arms and enthralled, and it would be so incredibly difficult to do anything but complete the longed-for journey and make her his.

After a mighty effort he tried to calm the storm they'd created. It was the last thing he wanted but once he'd had her he knew he'd never be able to resist again. He still wasn't sure he was the best person for Bella. At such a time in his life was he loving Bella or seeking comfort from the hurt of being excluded from his son's life? Amidst all his emotional confusion, could he really trust his feelings? He tried to concentrate on that thought but it receded in the heat of the moment.

Scott groaned and tried to break away as he recognised how close they were to total abandon. But Bella wouldn't let him. She held him with her hands on either side of his face, as if for them to break apart would terminate the world she'd finally found with him.

He could see the last of his control spinning out of reach, and he dug deeper to regain it. No matter what the cost, he had to know if she really wanted this.

'Are you sure, Bella?' He wrenched the words out against her mouth and she stilled for a moment as if she comprehended, but he didn't think she did. Then her tongue touched his with emboldened innocence and he felt the spear of intense pleasure shatter his gut into a million pieces. He had to kiss her back and the vortex swallowed him.

The next time he surfaced she was in his arms, soft and pliant against his chest as he strode to his bed. They were semi-naked and he leaned over her when he laid her across the quilt in front of him. Red hair fanned out behind her in a crinkled wave, and the tips of her creamy breasts spilled from the lace of her bra. She was everything he'd dreamed of and had never imagined holding. The briefest window of sanity opened and it was up to him to make the final effort.

'Bella?' He stared into her eyes until she focussed, and he saw the exact moment when she realised he had control back. 'We need to stop.'

'Don't even think about stopping!' she whispered,

and pulled his head down. He groaned and accepted that he'd lost and won and lost until he realised there was one more responsibility.

He reached for his wallet in his discarded trousers. The condom really did glow in the dark.

CHAPTER NINE

WHEN sanity returned, Bella lay snuggled in his arms and Scott stared at the ceiling. He could feel her body warm and sweet against his and he couldn't comprehend how they had come to this stage. All the years he'd wanted her, and now she rested in his arms as if she belonged there. He couldn't fool himself it would be for ever but for the moment it was worth grabbing and holding to cherish in the empty years to come.

He squeezed her against him and she burrowed into his chest and he thought he could die a happy man. But he didn't say it because he didn't think he would.

A short time later Bella stirred and edged away from under his encircling arm until she could sit up. He felt her rise from the bed and he stretched out his hand to detain her but unconsciously she evaded him. Even now, when his wildest dream had come true, he didn't know what she was thinking.

She stretched to reach his shirt that was lying in a scrunched heap near her foot and held it against her chest. The crickets chirped in the back yard and he could hear the sound of occasional traffic. She stood with her back to the bed and looked out into the lounge room where the music had finished. Thank goodness they hadn't turned the lights on. Mentally, he felt better in the dark.

The moon was rising so before he had to look at everything under a spotlight, he needed to think the events of the day through.

Bella walked away and he stared at the purity of line in the curve of her back. Then she was gone from his sight and he couldn't think of anything except the feeling of emptiness without Bella against him. It was as if he'd lost her all over again. He rolled back and stared at the ceiling again.

The responsibility for the last half-hour rested with both of them. But where did their future lie? What did she expect from him? He loved her too much to short-change her. He'd failed as a husband before, and failed as a father. If they had children together he'd be sixty before they left home. The picture chilled him. Maybe he should find and make peace with his own son before he risked his parenting skills on any children Bella might want.

The memory of the photograph in the other room haunted him, along with that crazy, improbable thought that had crossed his mind—long hair and piercings aside, the resemblance between Blake and himself in his youth was remarkable.

He pushed the thought from his mind. Bella deserved his full commitment, not just the part of him that didn't belong to the son he had to find. He needed more time so he could give her everything she deserved.

'Bella?'

She heard Scott's voice from the bedroom and she cast one more glance at the photograph before crossing the hall to slip back into the room. He stretched out his hand to draw her back to bed and she slipped under the sheet to nestle under his arm.

He lifted her fingers to his mouth and she closed her eyes at the reverence of his salute. It was the tenderness of his love-making that had undone her. Every caress had said Scott loved her. She didn't doubt that fact because it had been in his every searching kiss, every touch and in his superhuman efforts to prevent the one thing that she'd needed to feel whole again.

With relief, she became aware that any lingering disgust from last year's attack had dissolved and been replaced with the tenderness of her true love's consummation.

And she loved Scott. She always had. What came next should be simple, but she knew it wouldn't be. There would be a struggle to overcome his entrenched ideas of what she deserved in a husband.

'If you loved me, why waste twelve years that we could have been together? Why has it taken so long to get here, Scott?'

Bella's voice drifted across to him and Scott breathed in the scent of her skin one last time before he let her go. Every word she spoke was like a knife. This was what he'd been afraid of. She needed his total commitment. The whole man he'd never revealed to her. He was afraid she wouldn't find him the hero she expected him to be. 'Where do you think we are, Bella?'

He felt her shift onto her side and he turned his head to see her face close to his. The first of the lunar rays came in through the bedroom window and bathed the purity of her features and she was the moon goddess he was afraid of failing.

'I know you love me.' Bella's voice was firm with conviction. 'You've shown me in more ways than you can ever say and I won't believe you if you say you don't.'

'Of course I love you,' he said, and she sighed with relief. Then his voice lowered because the lies wouldn't come out in a strong voice. 'But I'm not sure of marriage or children or setting up house together or tying you to visiting me in the nursing home when I'm decrepit.'

She flinched and he felt the pain being dragged through his guts like an oversized grappling hook. Here he was again, wounding Bella for her own good. He hated it. He hated the whole bloody fiasco. And he almost wished she hated him so that he would never have to do this again. He sat up on the edge of the bed with his back to her.

'None of those things frighten me, Scott,' she said. 'So before you erect a wall between us...' she laid her hand on his arm '...I would like to know, if you weren't thinking marriage and commitment and children, what you were thinking when we made love.'

He refused to look at her. 'There was so much heat I didn't think of much at all. You stun me. The scent of you drives me out of my mind. There wasn't much room for deep and meaningful.'

Her laugh held a trace of bitterness. 'Why do you think I do that to you and you do it to me? As for chemistry driving us to abandon—I seem to remember it was more on my mind than yours.' She shook her head. 'You're lying. If that was all our *little romp*—' she watched him flinch at the words '—was to you, why did you try to stop it happening?'

At that he swung his feet over the edge of the bed and stood up, and the moonlight turned him into a silver stranger, strong-chested and implacable.

'You're not a child any more, Bella. Fairy-tales don't happen.' He stared at her. 'What we did may not have been the most sensible course for this stage in our relationship. I'm sorry I didn't realise that sooner.'

Bella couldn't believe he'd said that. 'Well, just so you know for future reference, your apology is not needed. I decide when and with whom I make love— it's my responsibility. From your comments it looks as though I took advantage of you. I believe what we have is beautiful and pure and if you're too frightened to reach for it I can't force you.' She slid out of the bed and collected her clothes.

Scott was still going to fight against something that should have been sorted out years ago. He couldn't deny that they created magic when they were together and she felt like screaming with frustration when he'd said it was all just proximity.

He loved her and finally she was sure of that. That in itself was liberating. She glanced back at him at the side of the bed and allowed herself a small mental hug at the memories of their time together and then walked from the room to phone a taxi.

She dressed and while she waited she put her head in her hands. How was she going to convince Scott that it was him she'd always wanted? Surely he didn't

believe she thought him too old. No fool could believe that. But what was she supposed to do? She
wouldn't give up. That was for sure. Today had been
a major step forward—as long as he didn't shut her
out.

Monday

Monday on the ward was busy, which was lucky as
there was little time for personal concerns once Bella
arrived for work.

A woman with an undiagnosed breech presentation
in labour had been booked for urgent Caesarean section for eight o'clock. Bella needed to ensure all was
ready for the patient to be transferred.

Rene Jackson had been at school a couple of years
ahead of Bella, and the two girls had played hockey
together.

Bella was thrilled to see her friend. 'Rene, I didn't
recognise your married name. It's great to see you.'

Rene, a petite blonde-haired woman, smiled at
Bella with relief. 'I'm so pleased you're on. Sharon
said you'll come with me to the theatre.' Her voice
shook. 'It's all been such a shock.'

Bella hugged her. 'Caesareans always are. The
scary thing is that between ten and twenty per cent
of women seem to end up with one.' She helped Rene
dissolve her nail polish with remover so that the
anaesthetist could see the colour of her nailbeds if he
needed to.

Rene chewed her lip. 'I'm worried about Jim, my
husband. What if he faints when the operation starts?'

Bella smiled. 'Not many husbands faint in Theatre. We set you up so that neither of you can see the gory bits. He'll sit in a chair beside your head and when your baby is born it's all worth it to be awake for the actual birth and to have your man beside you.'

Rene twisted her ring on her finger so Bella could tape it in place so that it wouldn't get caught on anything in Theatre. 'We talked about it and Jim is keen to be there for me.' She glanced at the travel clock on the bedside table. 'He should be here soon.'

As she spoke there was a knock on the door and a tall surprisingly young-looking man hastened in with a worried frown on his face and a huge bunch of roses in his hand. When he saw that all was normal in the room he visibly relaxed and came across to hug his wife. 'Sorry I'm late, baby. I wanted to get you flowers before you went in.'

Rene smiled mistily up at her hero and Bella slipped out to give them some privacy. It must be nice to be so sure you could declare your love to the world, she thought.

When she returned to prepare Rene for transfer to Theatre, Bella could see that Rene was even more nervous and Jim was downright terrified.

'Remember, you guys, even though you haven't done this before, we have! Lots of times. And we're very good at it.' The couple smiled and Bella helped Rene onto the theatre trolley for transport to the operating theatre.

'You walk beside Rene's head, Jim, and I'll walk on the other side. Pete, our orderly, is the engine.' Pete waved at the couple and the mood lightened despite the movement towards Theatre.

Theatre Sister met them at the door and good-naturedly grilled Rene on who she was and what she was there for.

Rene looked up at the circle of faces above her. 'Dr Rainford is going to find out what this big bump in my stomach is.' She smiled bravely and Jim looked like he wanted to cry with pride.

Theatre Sister produced the consent form and went through it all again with Rene and then they were through. Bella slipped away to change into her theatre scrubs and Pete took Jim into the surgeons' room to do the same.

By the time they returned to Rene, she was draped and in a sitting position.

Dr Knowles, the elderly anaesthetist, smiled at Jim. 'Now you're all here we can get started. If you'd like to hold her hand, Dad, I'll explain as I go.' Jim stood in front of his wife and she leaned her face into his chest.

'Right, then, Rene. I'm going to give you a local anaesthetic in your back first, and then the area will be numb. You won't feel the bigger needle or the little catheter that I leave behind to inject the anaesthetic into but you will feel some pushing and prodding.'

Rene nodded and Jim squeezed her hand. The whole procedure was completed ten minutes later when a long thick strip of sticking-plaster was placed over the tubing to keep it in place in the epidural space where the anaesthetic would bathe the nerves at that level and deaden sensation. By leaving a catheter in place, Dr Knowles could top up Rene with more anaesthetic if she needed it.

'My legs feel funny,' Rene said, and Dr Knowles nodded.

'They'll feel heavy and later when I check with some ice, you won't be able to feel the sensation of cold either.'

After a short while, Rene was moved onto the operating table and sterile green sheets were draped until she and Jim couldn't see her stomach any more.

'How are you going, you two?' Bella joined their little space for a moment before she had to get scrubbed.

'It feels weird to know they're doing things I can't feel,' Rene said, and Bella squeezed her shoulder.

'I know. But your baby will be here soon. I'll be back in a while and we'll gag all the people up the other end so Jim can announce what you've had. OK?' The two nodded and Bella ensured the resuscitation trolley was functioning.

She switched on the infant overhead heater and light on the resuscitation trolley.

She really had no part of the operation except to stand beside the assisting surgeon—in this case, Rohan—and wait for the baby to be born, when she would be in charge of any resuscitation required.

Because Rene hadn't actually gone long into labour and was under epidural anaesthetic and not general anaesthetic, the baby would be very unlikely to need any sort of resuscitation. So today was about as much parental contact in those first few minutes as possible.

Gloved and gowned, Bella stepped up to the operating table and Scott looked up. There was an aura between them that brought a blush to Bella's cheeks and she was glad that no one could see her face. His eyes met hers and while she couldn't tell what he was thinking, indifference wasn't the emotion. She'd never felt this way across the table from him before and she looked down to where she'd clasped her hands together to still the sudden tremor his presence caused. When she looked up again he was back at work. She stared down at the operation in case someone saw the confusion in her eyes.

She saw Rohan glance at the two of them and Bella could tell he'd decided that she and Scott had something going on. For him, he was surprisingly quiet.

But maybe that was because those last few seconds before the baby was born were always tense. The incision was made, the waters were broken and Scott had his hand inside Rene's abdomen. The baby's head was high in Rene's chest and Bella watched as first one foot and then the other and then two round little buttocks were eased out of the abdominal cavity, followed by the baby's chest.

'Breech is the only time you get to see what it is before you see who it is,' said Scott, and his eyes smiled as he met Bella's warning look. 'But we're not going to say it.' He slid the forceps in beside the baby's head and gently eased the last of the baby out.

Rohan clamped and cut the cord and handed the infant to Bella, who lightly suctioned baby's mouth and then scooted around to Rene and Jim with their baby in her arms. 'Well, Jim, what have you got?'

'It's a girl,' Jim said as the tears rolled down his face. He kissed his wife. 'You've given me a daughter, and she's beautiful like her mother. I want to call her Georgia Rene.'

When Georgia Rene had been cuddled, and with

some tenacious manoeuvring by Bella and long-suffering agreement by Scott, the baby was breastfed on the operating table as the operation went on. After the feed, Bella, Jim and Georgia went back to the ward to wait for Rene to return.

'Now I want you to sit in Rene's darkened room and cuddle your baby against your skin.' Jim obediently sat on the chair and held out his arms. 'Take your shirt off,' Bella said, and Jim stared at her.

Bella smiled at his confusion. 'If she'd been born normally she'd have been placed on her mother's skin. Because she was a Caesarean it doesn't mean she can't have that same feeling with her dad.'

Jim shrugged. 'I'm game. Compared to what Rene had to go through, I get the best part.' He took his naked daughter from Bella and cuddled her against his not inconsiderable chest, wrapped in a blanket. Bella left them and Jim explained to his daughter about the new world as they both waited for the most important woman in their lives to come back to them.

An hour later Scott came around to the ward to see Jim. Father and baby were dozing in the chair and Scott pulled the door shut after backing out of the room. He went in search of Bella.

'What on earth is going on in that room?' he asked. 'Jim's semi-naked and the baby is glued to his chest.'

Bella shook her head. 'Welcome to the new millennium, Dr Rainford. It's called father bonding. They tested babies and those warmed against either parent's skin warmed faster than those warmed in humidicribs.'

'I believe you but thousands wouldn't.'

Bella raised her eyebrows. 'I can produce the study, I'll get it off the internet tonight.'

To her surprise he said, 'I'll drop around.'

'Why?' she asked.

'We need to talk.' He didn't smile but she heaved a sigh of relief. He wasn't going to pretend last night had never happened.

'After seven, then,' she said, and he waved and left the ward.

Somehow the rest of the day was tinged with excitement and Bella flew through her work with single-minded precision. The day was busy as she spent time with Rene as the new mother settled back into the ward.

Bella bent the rules and suggested Jim stay the night in Rene's room as her personal nurse and nanny to his wife and their baby until Rene could move more easily. It was something Gladstone hadn't seen but was quite common in the birthing centre where Bella had worked in Sydney. There were advantages to being the boss, Bella thought with a wry grin.

Come five o'clock, she walked out to Blake's car with a light step and she couldn't believe she'd caught up on all the administrative work that had accumulated while she'd been away as well.

By seven o'clock she'd organised the household accounts and even the linen cupboard. Aunt Sophie came out of her room and stopped her in the hallway with a poke.

'Are you on speed or something?'

Bella stopped and looked at her aunt and then she burst out laughing. 'No. I'm just feeling very efficient today and I'm capitalising on the feeling while it's there.'

'Balderdash. Something's going on.' She snapped her sparse white eyebrows together and stared at her niece. The doorbell rang and Bella looked at the door and then back at her aunt.

Sophie's lip twitched. 'Expecting someone?' She cackled. 'I think I'll get the door.'

Bella narrowed her eyes at her aunt and Sophie cackled again. 'Or I might just go back into my room and watch the next race.' She ambled away but Bella could hear her chuckling. The doorbell rang again and Vivie came out of the kitchen to answer it and saw Bella. She looked from Bella to the door. 'Did you want me to get that?'

Bella felt like stamping her foot. Now it was a production. Sometimes she did wish she lived on her own. She plastered a smile on her face. 'No, thank you, Vivie. I'll get it.'

Vivie nodded, disconcerted, and then shrugged and walked back into the kitchen.

Bella walked across towards the door before the person on the other side hit the doorbell again, but she was too late.

It rang and Blake came bolting down the stairs to get it just as Bella opened the door and father and son were left staring at each other.

CHAPTER TEN

IT WAS the first time Scott had seen the new Blake. Short-haired and shaven, it was as if the young man from the photo on Scott's mantelpiece had stepped down into real life. Bella saw the exact moment that Scott confirmed the resemblance between himself and Bella's boarder. He shot an accusing look at Bella as if she'd known all along.

The younger man stared from Scott to Bella and the sudden tension between the two sharpened his senses. His eyes widened as Scott took a step towards him.

'Michael?' At Scott's question he backed away from the door.

Blake looked shocked and angry and spun away through the kitchen. A few seconds later Bella heard the back door shut and then the sound of his car revving as he drove away.

She sighed. 'I'm sorry about that. It was a misunderstanding.'

Scott stood still in the doorway and didn't say anything, just looked at Bella as if it was all her fault she hadn't told him.

'Please, come in, Scott. I know what you're thinking, that Blake is your son. I agree it's a strong possibility but I don't know for sure. I just had suspicions.' Surely, especially after last night, he wasn't going to shut her out of this.

Scott stared at her for a moment and then nodded. 'Considering you are the first to say it out loud, I'd say it's pretty clear that Blake is my son.'

Bella led the way through to the study and Scott sat gingerly in the big chair until he realised his own son had fixed it and he could sit in it normally. His mouth hardened at the irony of it.

'Am I jumping to conclusions?' he said.

Bella shook her head. She tried to block out that he hadn't said, Are *we* jumping to conclusions? 'I don't think so. Apart from the fact that he looks just like you twenty years ago, Blake's middle name is Michael, he's twenty, the people he knew as his parents died in the last year and he's an only child from Sydney. It all fits.'

'So how did he end up here?'

She smiled gently. 'At a guess I'd say he came to see what sort of man his father was.'

'An arrogant sort.' He winced. 'I haven't been very complimentary about him.'

'There's time for that. He's a wonderful young man and a joy to have around. But he's confused. Let him meet you halfway.'

Scott ran his hands through his hair. 'As long as he doesn't kill himself in that car.'

'Welcome to parenthood.' Bella smiled. 'You really have it in for his car, don't you?'

'Actually, I have some good memories of that car.' He met her eyes and there was a brief moment of intimacy before he dashed her sudden hopes when his mind returned to his son. She could feel the wall he erected between them. She wasn't invited into this area and Bella tried to contain the hurt that was spreading through her. He confirmed it when he stood up. 'I'll go. I need to think about the events of the evening.'

'Maybe I could help.' She sounded pathetic but Bella couldn't help herself. She hated to see him in pain and she hated that he didn't think she could help. She stood as well and followed him to the door. 'Don't be too hard on yourself. You couldn't have known.'

'Thank you, Bella.' He made no move to kiss her. 'I'll see you tomorrow.'

She watched him walk down the path without looking back. Maybe this wasn't going to work out after all if he could shut her out so easily.

Later that evening she heard Blake's car pull into the garage but he didn't seek her out. Like his father. Bella sighed and went to bed. Reality bites.

Maybe she needed a BITE ME sticker on her forehead.

Tuesday

When Bella went down to breakfast, Blake was there.

'I owe you an apology, Bella. I shouldn't have left both of you like that.' He met her eyes. 'I suppose you guessed I was Michael the day after you hurt your ankle.' He shrugged. 'You had to do what you thought was right.'

'Thank you, Blake. I appreciate that.' She poured her cereal into the bowl. 'But I didn't tell him.'

Blake stared at her and she shook her head. 'He came to the conclusion after he saw you and you left. It will take time but you're both special people, I'm sure you'll work it out.'

Vivie looked from one to the other. Bella continued with her breakfast as she listened to Blake discuss his father with Vivie.

She was glad he had someone else he could talk it over with. 'There may be one extra for tea tonight, Vivie.' Vivie nodded and didn't ask who.

'Your car is ready.' Blake gestured to the refrigerator. 'Key's on the fridge.'

'Wonderful, thank you, Blake. Though I'm going to miss that Torana of yours.'

Blake laughed. 'I think you'll find yours goes a little better than you remember. I've given it a birthday and it doesn't seem to feel its age any more.'

Bella looked up. 'Will heads turn when I drive down the street, do you think?'

'Unlikely,' he said dryly, and he looked so like Scott that she felt like giving him a hug. But more because she needed one than he did.

Later that morning, Bella helped Rene into the shower while Jim went home to change his clothes. Rene's intravenous line had been removed and a waterproof dressing protected her suture line.

'You're standing so straight, Rene, considering your operation was only yesterday.'

Rene walked carefully to the bathroom. 'I don't

have as much pain as I'd expected. I'm stiff from lying in bed more than actually sore from the cut.'

Bella nodded. 'I've noticed that the women who have their Caesareans performed under epidural block seem to bounce back sooner than those who have a general anaesthetic.'

'I don't want to compare them to find out,' Rene said.

Bella smiled. 'OK.'

Twenty minutes later, when Rene was back sitting in the chair, hair combed and freshly made up, she sighed as she gazed at her sleeping baby. 'I'm so happy.'

'You have a beautiful daughter,' Bella agreed as she repacked Rene's bathroom bag.

'Jim is wonderful. I can't believe I fought against marrying him for so long.'

Bella sat on the edge of the bed to listen. 'So how much age difference is there between you two?'

'Ten years.' Rene shrugged and Bella blinked. She'd realised Jim was younger than Rene but ten years was close to the difference between Scott and herself.

'He just wore me down.'

Then her face sobered. 'One day I lost one of my girlfriends to cancer. She was my age. Life is too short not to grab happiness when you can.' She smiled the smile of a contented woman. 'I was a fool. Wasted time.'

Bella nodded but Rene's words played on her mind, and when Scott came for his round she couldn't help commenting about the couple.

'Rene and Jim are thrilled with their new baby.'

Bella handed the chart to Scott and he glanced at his patient's observations on the graph.

'They're a lovely couple,' he said.

'Funny how the age difference doesn't seem to bother them.'

He glanced across quickly but Bella's face was expressionless. 'Was there a point to that comment?' He said.

Bella looked blandly back. 'Should there be?'

Bella picked up the charts and shuffled them. She chose one out of the stack and opened it on the way down the corridor. 'I'm happy with Melissa's Tina. She's nine days old and taking all her feeds at the breast now.'

They entered Melissa's room and the noise that was coming from such a tiny baby made Scott smile. 'She certainly sounds vigorous.' He looked at the feed chart at the end of the bed as Melissa changed her daughter's nappy. As soon as she finished the baby stopped crying and they all smiled.

'I hear that Tina is doing well, Melissa. Are you happy with her?'

'She's great.' Melissa rocked the cot. 'This morning she hasn't had any tube feeds. When do you think we could go home?'

Scott pulled the stethoscope from around his neck and listened to Tina's heartbeat. Then he watched the rise and fall of her chest. 'She looks and sounds great. We'll weigh her tomorrow and if she's still over five pounds, you can go home Thursday afternoon.'

'Woo-hoo.' Melissa's grin nearly split her face. 'Can't wait.'

Scott smiled and they moved into Rene's room

where all was well. Rene nursed her baby confidently and Scott enthused over Georgia. He promised to come back the next day to check on their progress.

After Scott left, Bella went back to take Rene's temperature and her friend tapped Bella's arm.

'So how long have you and Dr Rainford had something going on?'

Bella looked away. 'We don't!'

'Yeah, right. I know that look in a man's eye and you're not immune to him either.' She looked at Bella measuringly. 'You'll have to chase him.'

Bella charted the observations. 'I tried that and it didn't work. I'm not much of a chaser. It's really not my style.'

Rene shook her head. 'Maybe when we were young it wasn't your style but I can see you've changed. You've suffered and you're stronger than you've ever been. Don't be afraid to push for something you want—even if it frightens you.'

She twisted the wedding ring on her finger. 'Jim didn't give up and I'm so glad he didn't.' She shrugged. 'I think it's easier for the younger one to push—because the older partner feels that they're getting the best of the bargain.'

She laughed. 'I know I thought everyone was going to say, "Look at that old hag with that young stud." And I'm still sensitive, but nothing on what I was, and I'm happier than I've ever been. If I'd kept being stubborn about what other people might think, I'd have missed out on the best years of my life and a love that I can't imagine not having.'

Bella felt the tears spring to her eyes and she

hugged her friend. 'Thank you, Rene. I appreciate your honesty. And I will think about it.'

'You make sure you do.' There was a knock on the door and Bella excused herself as Jim came in to be with his wife and daughter.

She saw Rene wink and Bella smiled as she walked up the corridor. Maybe there was a ray of hope. Maybe she'd been selfish, not giving credence to Scott's fears. She tried to imagine how she would feel if Scott was Blake's age and she was in love with him. It was a thought-provoking concept.

Bella imagined falling in love with Blake, so young and naïve from where she stood at thirty. She imagined the raised eyebrows if she ran off with him. Maybe Scott hadn't been so out of line after all.

Even if she could remove the ten years of her own that had passed and be twenty and innocent again, she'd still want Scott. His maturity and confidence were exactly what she wanted. He had so much to offer her and she had so much to offer both Scott and his son.

All she had to do was make it happen.

At the end of the shift her car drove itself past Scott's gate and Bella hesitated over inviting him to tea. There hadn't been an appropriate time at work to float the notion to him but she could just suggest it and see what he said.

When he didn't answer the doorbell she followed the path around the side of the house, a bit like a lemming bent on nirvana. He wasn't on the verandah and she hesitated before turning onto the path to the workshop. The sound of rhythmic planing from the shed drifted among the trees and confirmed his presence.

When she took the fork under the leopard tree Bella could see him and she stopped and leaned against the trunk to watch him work through the open door. He planed smoothly and the sight was as she'd imagined once before.

Layer after layer, he worked like some old-fashioned craftsman from the past, no hurry, just sweeping strokes that pared the imperfections from the wood. A faint sheen of sweat glowed on his bare chest as he concentrated on the wood under his hands and carefully skimmed the roughness from the length of wood. Curls of shavings lay scattered around him like streamers at a monotone farewell party. She watched the bunching and relaxing of his muscles and her mouth dried as she remembered the feel and strength of him against her.

He laid the smooth piece down and picked up another. She must have made a sound because he looked up and unerringly focussed on where she stood.

The clatter of the wood as he tossed it onto the bench seemed discordant as their eyes held across the path and her head swam until she remembered to breathe.

'What do you want, Bella?' There was a caution in his voice that didn't correlate with what they'd shared. She wished she'd known what had gone wrong. But she wasn't here for herself.

'Nothing you don't want to give.' The words lay between them for a moment before she shrugged them off. 'I enjoy watching you work.' She paused but he didn't comment so she went on, 'I'm here to talk about Blake.'

He pulled his shirt on and came towards her and she couldn't help the leap in her pulse rate. 'Let's sit on the verandah,' he said, and waited for her to precede him up the path.

A cane table was set up beside the bridge and he gestured for her to sit. The sound of the water as it trickled over the stones was very peaceful but it didn't help the tension between them.

She sank into the chair and all she could think about was the last time they'd been here.

He said, 'How was Blake this morning?'

Bella ignored the flash of disappointment and refused to be intimidated by the fact that he towered over her. She crossed her ankles, and assumed a relaxed pose and told herself that he couldn't tell that was all it was. 'Fine,' she said. 'He regrets that he rushed away and confirmed he was your son. I explained that you had guessed yourself. Perhaps you should come for tea tonight?'

Scott turned away and gazed out over the garden. 'It will be awkward.'

'No more awkward than this,' she said. He looked at her from under his brows and a twisted smile acknowledged the hit.

'True, but I didn't ask you to come here.'

She forced herself to remain seated when she wanted to get up and shake him. She needed to take a grip on the truth that he didn't want her closeness at this time.

She raised her chin. 'It will be more awkward if

you don't make a move. Blake may think you don't want to know him.'

'You're right.' Scott sighed. 'Thank you. What time?'

'Six-thirty, if you can make it. Aunt Sophie likes to eat early.'

Scott groaned. 'Can't wait for Sophie's comments.'

'You'll survive.' Bella stood and he gestured for her to go through the house and out the front door. Neither of them glanced into the lounge room and he was careful not to touch her.

When Scott arrived that evening, he maintained the wall between himself and Bella. Blake was in the yard, working on his car, and Bella showed Scott through the house and out the back door to talk to his son. After all, she told herself, that was the only reason he'd come.

Vivie and Bella hung back behind the curtain in the kitchen and watched from afar, but they couldn't hear what was said.

They watched Scott hold out his hand for his son to shake. Blake hesitated for a moment but then they briefly shook on their relationship.

For Scott it was a strange moment. This young man in front of him was of his own genes. Matured in some distant world that he knew nothing about and had contributed nothing to. How could Blake do anything but hate him?

'I don't hate you.' Scott felt the trickle of superstition down his neck at Blake's comment.

'Well, we must have some connection if you can read my thoughts. Unless I've got it tattooed on my forehead.' At the word tattoo they both looked at the scorpion on Blake's wrist and smiled at each other.

'So, am I what you expected?' Blake's own insecurities were there as well, and Scott shrugged.

'I didn't know what to expect.' He glanced up at the house. 'Bella seems to like you.'

'Bella is awesome. How come you two aren't together?'

'I let your mother down, and Bella deserves more.'

Blake screwed up his face in disbelief. 'That was twenty years ago. What's the real reason? She said you think you're too old for her.'

Scott winced. 'There's that.'

'More crap. But it's none of my business.'

Scott laughed. 'So is this what it means to have a son? They tell you when you're being a fool.'

Blake shrugged. 'Anyone could tell you that.'

Scott smiled again and suddenly it wasn't so frightening to meet his son. Blake's expectations were nowhere near as harsh as the ones Scott had for himself. Maybe that had been his problem all along. Maybe he should listen to Bella's expectations before he convinced himself he couldn't meet them. Maybe he *was* all kinds of fool. But that was for later.

Watching, Vivie and Bella sighed in relief. Both men looked under the bonnet of the car and once they heard Scott laugh. Thank God, Bella thought. 'Has Blake said much to you, Vivie?'

'I think Blake's getting used to the idea.' Vivie said. 'But he doesn't understand what happened between his real parents.'

Bella nodded. 'From what I can gather, I don't think Dr Rainford understands what happened to his marriage. He never knew about Blake until Blake wrote to him.'

Vivie shook her head. 'So Blake said. I hope it works out for them.'

'Me, too,' said Bella. The men didn't stay long down at the Torana and Bella and Vivie left their vantage point before they were caught spying.

When everyone had assembled for the meal, there was an uneasy silence. Sophie dived in. 'So? How does it feel to have dinner with your son, Dr Rainford?'

Thanks, Aunt Sophie, Bella thought with a groan, but Scott managed. He plastered a smile on his face and looked across at Blake. 'Pretty scary, if you want the truth.'

Unconsciously he'd picked the right thing to say, and Bella saw Blake shoot a glance at his father. Then he smiled and chipped in.

'I'm with you there.'

They all laughed. The conversation flowed more smoothly after that. Maybe Sophie had been right to bring it out in the open.

Scott and Blake didn't avoid each other in the discussions but they had a long way to go before rapport was established.

At least they had a chance of things working out in the end, Bella thought as Scott made no effort to single her out in the conversation.

When Scott had gone, again without making any moves to include Bella in his private life, she closed the door after him and leaned against it.

'So what's changed between you two?' Sophie's words came out of the doorway to her right, and Bella pushed herself off the door and went in to see her aunt.

She sat down beside Sophie and sighed. 'I thought we had a new understanding but he's become more distant…' since we made love, she thought '…since he found out about Blake,' she said.

'Give the man time. It must be a huge change to find you have family. He's not used to people caring what happens to him, and that includes you. He's been so busy looking after everyone else he probably feels it's wrong to be self-absorbed. It's a nuisance but men are pretty painful anyway.'

Bella considered her aunt's explanation. Maybe Scott *was* just having problems with change. He had been a little warmer before he'd left. The idea lifted her spirits. 'You're a very wise woman, Aunt Sophie.' Bella kissed her aunt's wrinkled cheek. 'Don't ever let me forget it.'

'I won't. Now, go to bed so you can knock his socks off with sex appeal tomorrow.'

'That didn't work,' Bella muttered as she left.

'Practice makes perfect,' her aunt called, and Bella had to laugh. For a spinster, Sophie delighted in the risqué.

CHAPTER ELEVEN

Wednesday

SEX appeal, eh? Bella had mused on her aunt's words overnight and a vague plan formed when she woke on Wednesday morning. It was time to stop hiding her femininity and bring out the big guns. Thanks to the other night, despite Scott's behaviour since then, she knew she was cherished, and it was time to use that power.

Bella gave herself an extra spray of perfume after her shower and donned her prettiest underwear for confidence. As she stood in front of the mirror she chose a soft red lipstick rather than her usual pink and left one more button undone on the front of her shirt. She clasped her hair back with combs instead of her usual bun, and it was amazing what a difference it made.

Blake whistled appreciatively when she walked into the kitchen, and she burst out laughing. 'Thank you. I'm not sure what I would have done if nobody had noticed.'

'What's the occasion?' Blake's question could have been awkward but Bella was feeling brave.

'I'm trying to seduce your father.' She listened to that sentence and shook her head. 'Actually, I'm going to seduce your father.'

'Watch out, old man.' Blake grinned and Vivie covered her mouth to giggle.

Bella pretended to frown. 'You're lucky you have good genes! He's not as old as you think.'

Blake shuddered as he sat down at the table. 'Too much information. I'm trying to get my head around him as it is.'

Bella hid her smile and patted his arm. 'I know. I think you're both doing as well as can be expected in the circumstances.' She poured her breakfast cereal and changed the subject.

'I heard there was a job going at the hospital in the maintenance department. Maybe you could ring and see if it's true.'

Blake shot his head up and grinned. 'What's the number? Doing what? What qualifications do I need?'

Bella passed across a slip of paper. 'I'd wait until eight-thirty but you should be able to get onto them and find out after that.'

Later on that morning, Scott arrived to do his round on the maternity ward. Bella had forced down the butterflies and met him at the desk with a sultry smile.

Scott frowned. Bella looked different this morning. His eyes strayed to the discreet gap in her blouse and stayed there until she covered her cleavage with the charts.

He heard her laugh and the gentle sound drew an absent smile from him. 'Are you coming on the round, Scott?' she said, and he blinked and refocussed on the rest of the world.

'Sorry. I don't seem to be plugged in this morning.'

'So I see.' She leaned over and flicked his collar

straight and then moved serenely up the corridor. The scent of her perfume lingered around him and he had difficulty concentrating on work as he followed her. Even her skirt seemed tighter today.

She stood on the other side of Melissa's bed directly opposite him and when he glanced across she moistened her lips with her tongue and all his promises to himself that he'd stay immune to Bella flew out the window. Then he realised that she was teasing him deliberately, and a slow smile curved his lips. He shook his head at what it must have cost her to choose that path.

He'd been such a fool to worry about age when what they had transcended all barriers. Hell, she made him feel younger than the twelve years between them. He had to acknowledge that Bella had him going like a randy sixteen-year-old and it was very distracting.

He gave in to the dreams he'd never believed in and accepted that he had no defence if she was determined to seduce him. Thank God.

He returned her look with a molten look of his own that promised all manner of forbidden pleasures if she so desired. He watched her eyes widen and a pink flush stained her cheeks. He restrained his smile.

Melissa, absorbed in calming her baby, missed the byplay and when young Tina had stopped crying Scott forced himself to concentrate on the discharge plans for his tiniest patient.

When they left Melissa's room, they passed an empty two-bedded room and Bella steered him around the corner and into the vacant bathroom. 'I want to show you something,' she said, and flicked on the light and pulled the door shut behind them. It was a very small room.

Bella watched him look around and then back at her, and his slow, sexy smile warmed her soul. 'And what are you up to today, Bella?'

Bella could feel her heart thumping and the sound seemed to fill the tiny room. He was back with her. Whatever cold and lonely place he'd been hiding in, he'd managed to escape. She licked dry lips and then realised what she'd done. It worked anyway.

He slid his arms around her and lowered his mouth to hers. 'You are an incredibly sexy lady, do you know that?' he murmured as he kissed her.

She closed her eyes and leaned into him, briefly pulling away to mumble, 'I'm trying,' before she pressed herself back against him.

'I guess what you're saying is we didn't have a one-night stand the other night.'

'Mmm,' she said against his mouth.

'And that we should really spend more time together like this?'

'Mmm.' She twisted her fingers through his hair.

Scott groaned and deepened the kiss for several earth-shattering seconds and then pulled away.

'I've been a fool but this isn't the place to tell you how. Tonight. My place. I'll pick you up at six.' And he put her gently from him and opened the door to usher her out. It was difficult to hide the awareness between them, though they tried.

Rene winked at Bella as she left the room after Scott's round. The rest of the day passed in a dream for Bella.

*   *   *

Half an hour later in Scott's surgery, things had become even more bizarre. His first patient was someone he'd least expected to see.

Aunt Sophie hobbled in and sat in front of his desk like an avenging witch. She pointed her bony finger at his chest and stabbed the air. 'I want to see you.'

Scott looked at the old lady warily, still amazed that she'd ventured out of the house. 'How can I help you, Sophie?'

'It's me that's going to help you, sonny, though, goodness knows, you don't deserve it the way you fumble around the point.'

She shook her head and her neck made tiny cracking noises with the movement. Scott winced at her audible arthritis. Sophie ignored it. 'Will you stop this rot you two are going on with? She loves you. You love her. I know it. You know it. Everyone else knows it. For goodness sake, whip her away and do something about it.'

Scott bit his lip. Sophie was incredible and he admired her all the more for the effort it must have taken to get her here. But she expected an answer. 'I don't think kidnapping is really my style,' Scott said patiently.

Sophie pretended to spit and Scott laughed out loud.

'Look, Sophie, I can see I've been a fool and you're right. I do love Bella, have always loved Bella, and I'd already decided to do something about it. OK? I appreciate your effort and you've been outrageous enough for today. I will think long and hard about your suggestion.'

He helped her stand and she leaned on her stick

more than she leaned on him. When he opened the door, Blake rose from one of the waiting-room chairs and came over to shake his father's hand. He met Blake's eyes and they both smiled over the top of Sophie's head. It was the first spontaneous acknowledgement between them and it felt good. Today was turning into an amazing day.

Blake lowered his voice. 'Then I'll see you at your wedding?'

Scott smiled. 'If she'll have me.'

His son rolled his eyes. 'As if not.' He helped Sophie as she began her journey across the room.

Taking Bella away wasn't feasible, but there was no reason they couldn't arrange something along the lines of a romantic surprise. Unfortunately it was only Wednesday and they had work tomorrow—although he was sure Rohan and Abbey would help him with that.

The thought made him smile. Maybe he was lightening up.

He wandered into his partner's room between patients, and it was surprisingly easy to rearrange his and Bella's schedule tomorrow. In fact, he ended up with the rest of the afternoon off to prepare his campaign. Rohan practically marched him off the premises and banned him from the practice until Friday morning.

When Bella walked into Scott's house that evening, it was filled with spring flowers and there was a huge banner hanging across the room. SCOTT LOVES BELLA!

She turned to look at Scott and her eyes filled with

tears. He'd said he'd tell her tonight and she'd been too nervous to dream it might really happen.

The scent was heavenly and she moved from vase to vase. The table outside on the verandah was set with crystal and lace.

There was a small box with a red satin ribbon at her place at the table and Bella turned to face the man she loved. He drew her into his arms and she felt the rumble in his chest against her cheek as he spoke.

'I'm sorry, Bella. I've been a fool. I finally realised that my expectations of what I couldn't give you had blinded me to what I can. I was a fool twelve years ago and nearly a fool again.' She shook her head because, since her conversation with Rene, she could see his old dilemmas.

He went on because he had to make her understand what had looked like reluctance on his part. 'I love you. I was willing to sacrifice my happiness and dreams for you, but I have no right to sacrifice yours.'

He cradled her shoulders. 'That night we were together was the most amazing night of my life. I never told you that and I should have. But it brought home to me that I had so many things unresolved. You were so giving and I needed more time to ensure I could give you everything you deserved before I committed myself to you.'

He drew her against his chest and she could hear the thump of his heart. 'I see now I was crazy,' he said. 'I should have shared my fears with you. Trusted you to help me.'

Bella spoke into his shirt. 'What were you afraid of, Scott?'

'I've failed as a husband before, and didn't make

it as a father. I thought you deserved my full commitment, not just the part of me that didn't belong to the son I had to find. I didn't even know if finding him would change me for the worse.'

He let her go and looked into her face. 'I should have known you would help me there, too.'

He drew her towards the table. 'I don't know what the future holds, but I do know I will always love you. I won't lock you out again. Will you marry me, Bella? Spend the rest of your life with me?' He took her hand and stroked her fingers as he waited for her response.

Bella stared up at him. This man she'd loved for so long was finally ready to celebrate their future together. It was unbelievable but she wasn't going to be the one who doubted now.

'Yes. Please. I love you, Scott. I've always loved you.'

He leaned forward and their lips met, and the tenderness and delight was there for both of them. A long while later he raised his head. 'That little show you put on in the ward was pretty enlightening.' He grinned wickedly and Bella blushed.

'I've bought us a present,' he said, and drew her along the verandah, down the stairs and along the path to his workshop. When she entered, Bella's eyes were drawn to the stylish sofa piled with pillows that had been placed against one wall of the shed. Beside it on a small table rested a beaded bottle of champagne, cooling in ice, and two glasses.

'I decided we needed somewhere soft in my workshop for you to sit when I work down here. You never know. The scent of freshly shaved wood might act as an aphrodisiac on my future wife.' He grinned as Bella curled up on the lounge to try it out.

Her smile was sultry. 'Do you think I'll disturb you?'

'Permanently,' he growled, and leaned down to nibble her ear. 'Don't ever stop.'

She laughed and then he kissed her and the champagne was forgotten as they found more enthralling things to do.

CHAPTER TWELVE

THE wedding was huge.

Abbey, magnificent as matron of honour, caught the best man's eye across the pulpit and blew her husband a kiss as they both remembered their own vows.

Kirsten, finally back from Saudi Arabia in time to be bridesmaid, grinned at such public displays of affection from her staid sister, but then a hush fell over the church.

Bella's entry stunned the congregation as she swayed like a radiant angel, complete with veil and floating dress, down the aisle to the man she loved. When she reached Scott's side, her husband-to-be clasped her hand as if he would never let her go.

The music swelled and then the words flowed around them and everyone heard their responses clear and true. All too soon it was over.

Scott's heart was full with the wonder of his blessings. Beautiful Bella, his new wife. His son, tall and proud beside him. His best friend and his new sisters-in-law. And a new beginning where he would make up for all the years he and Bella had missed. The tiredness he'd felt for years was gone and in its place was a thirst for love and life and all the dreams and joys of their lives to come.

'I love you, Bella Rainford,' he whispered in her ear.

Bella turned her face and kissed him. 'And I love you, my husband.'

They faced their friends and family and joyfully walked the rose-strewn carpet to a new life together.

Modern Romance™
...seduction and
passion guaranteed

Tender Romance™
...love affairs that
last a lifetime

Medical Romance™
...medical drama
on the pulse

Historical Romance™
...rich, vivid and
passionate

Sensual Romance™
...sassy, sexy and
seductive

Blaze Romance™
...the temperature's
rising

27 new titles every month.

Live the emotion

MILLS & BOON®

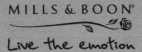

MILLS & BOON®

Live the emotion

Medical Romance™

DOCTORS IN FLIGHT *by Meredith Webber*

Dr Hillary Green never wanted to work in the Outback – and now she's in the Flying Obs and Gynae Service, taking tiny planes to rural hospitals, along with a boss who hates women registrars! Well, Hillary doesn't like him either – even if his touch does send needles of excitement shooting up her arm!

SAVING DR TREMAINE *by Jessica Matthews*

Paramedic Annie McCall might be beautiful and exceptionally caring, but she's also accident-prone! Someone has to watch over her – and Jared Tremaine, Hope City's handsome emergency physician, finds himself doing the job. But when Jared has an accident, and Annie volunteers to watch over *him*, the chemistry between them is impossible to ignore!

THE SPANISH CONSULTANT *by Sarah Morgan*

Spanish A&E consultant Jago Rodriguez was shocked to see Katy Westerling again – she still haunted his dreams eleven years on from their affair. Jago was convinced she hadn't changed, and was furious when he discovered she was their new doctor! But even their mutual mistrust could not hold back desire…

On sale 5th March 2004

Available at most branches of WHSmith, Tesco, Martins, Borders, Eason, Sainsbury's and all good paperback bookshops.

0204/03a

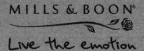

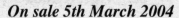

A Mother's Day Gift

A collection of brand-new romances just for you!

Margaret Way

Anne Ashley

Lucy Monroe

On sale 5th March 2004

Available at most branches of WHSmith, Tesco, Martins, Borders, Eason, Sainsbury's and all good paperback bookshops.

MILLS & BOON®

Live the emotion

The Elizabethan Season

A brand-new collection of sparkling historical romances

Volume 1 on sale from 5th March 2004

4 Books
and a surprise gift!

We would like to take this opportunity to thank you for reading this Mills & Boon® book by offering you the chance to take FOUR more specially selected titles from the Medical Romance™ series absolutely FREE! We're also making this offer to introduce you to the benefits of the Reader Service™—

- ★ FREE home delivery
- ★ FREE gifts and competitions
- ★ FREE monthly Newsletter
- ★ Books available before they're in the shops
- ★ Exclusive Reader Service discount

Accepting these FREE books and gift places you under no obligation to buy; you may cancel at any time, even after receiving your free shipment. Simply complete your details below and return the entire page to the address below. *You don't even need a stamp!*

YES! Please send me 4 free Medical Romance books and a surprise gift. I understand that unless you hear from me, I will receive 6 superb new titles every month for just £2.60 each, postage and packing free. I am under no obligation to purchase any books and may cancel my subscription at any time. The free books and gift will be mine to keep in any case.

M4ZEE

Ms/Mrs/Miss/Mr ....Initials..................................
BLOCK CAPITALS PLEASE

Surname..

Address..

....

....Postcode ....

Send this whole page to:
UK: The Reader Service, FREEPOST CN81, Croydon, CR9 3WZ
EIRE: The Reader Service, PO Box 4546, Kilcock, County Kildare (stamp required)

Offer not valid to current Reader Service subscribers to this series. We reserve the right to refuse an application and applicants must be aged 18 years or over. Only one application per household. Terms and prices subject to change without notice. Offer expires 30th May 2004. As a result of this application, you may receive offers from Harlequin Mills & Boon and other carefully selected companies. If you would prefer not to share in this opportunity please write to The Data Manager at the address above.

Mills & Boon® is a registered trademark owned by Harlequin Mills & Boon Limited.
Medical Romance™ is being used as a trademark.
The Reader Service™ is being used as a trademark.